UNDER THE HILL

First Published 15th June 2018
Copyright © Rachel V. Knox, 2018

The right of Rachel V. Knox to be identified as author of this work has been asserted in accordance with the Copyright, Designs and Patents Act 1988.

All rights reserved. No part of this book may be reproduced in any form or by any electronic or mechanical means, including information storage and retrieval systems, without permission in writing from the author, except by reviewers, who may quote brief passages in a review.

ISBN: 9781980931010

Cover art designer: CreativeGerman on Fiverr
Cover image: depositphotos.com

For my daughter,
Holly

The author wishes to stress that outside of known historical fact, such as Lloyd George's speech at Gwylfa Hiraethog in 1908, this is primarily a work of historical fiction.

House Under the Hill

Rachel V. Knox

1

March 1954

A piece of masonry falls in the north wing, bounds once over the moss-covered turf and colonises the shade with other crumbling specimens of its kind. It's that child again, her fingers picking away at anything cracked or loose. She's a small creature with spider-like curls squashed against her crown by the wool hat she wears. She writes on fallen roof tiles using sharp bits of flinty stone held cack-handed, always her name—Alis, followed by the date.

Chickens are living in the library, while the family live in the servants' quarters. The fowls peck at the red carpet that was once stepped on by the brogues of the Prince of Wales and roost in the empty shelves close to where Lloyd George discussed Home Rule with the Viscount. Chickens, princes, and prime ministers are all the same to me, but I miss the Viscount and his daughter. She used to play the piano and the harp; nowadays I have to make the music myself.

The bobble-hatted girl has finished defacing fallen tiles and has come inside. She wants to get into the library and pushes at the swollen door, but it's stuck fast. She keeps trying, throwing herself at the splintered surface of what was once a fine oak-panelled door. Using quick bursts of strength, with rests in between, she perseveres. The rusted hinges groan. After several more pushes, when she's quite out of breath, she falls through the door and looks up in surprise as she regains her feet and takes in the mist that flows in through the broken windows. Does she notice how the plaster has fallen away around the lintels? This is what happens to houses that aren't maintained. Water is our worst enemy; once it gets in, the mischief begins. Alis can see—if she cares to look—my rotting floorboards and the warped panelling that is beginning to break free of the wall, the blackened remnants of a Persian rug, mildewed books stuck together on the dust-covered shelves, their spines rupturing, and wallpaper unpeeling from the walls, a whole sheet at a time.

If the holes around my windows and my roof's disrepair aren't sorted out soon, my demise will be certain. But what's this? The mother is packing their things into boxes.

'We should buy some bread before the snow comes,' says Alis's mother.

'Too late,' the child laughs.

The mother frowns at the child's delight, but stops packing and joins Alis at the window of the lounge, where they watch a cloudburst of snow drifting in from the east.

'I won't be able to go to school,' says Alis happily.

'It might stop,' says her mother, 'it wasn't forecast to be heavy until next week.'

'It won't.'

'The snow plough will open the road.'

'But we don't live near to the road,' says the girl. 'And there'll be drifts too deep to walk in.'

'We'll see. Take your hat off and let your head breathe.'

'But I want to go out.'

'No, you can't.'

'Please Mam.'

'Wait until your father comes in. I have to make phone calls.'

It hasn't taken them long to pack their belongings because they don't have much. A lot of the furniture will stay because it isn't theirs. It belonged to others that lived here before. The entourage of servants that used to come up from Buckinghamshire used these same wardrobes and dressers, the dining table, the high-backed chairs, and the gas lamps. They slept on the metal framed beds and listened to the winds howling outside, drank cheap wine and played poker. Another family lived here then; they were known as the Kearleys when they first came.

Hudson Kearley was married to Selina. As well as being an effective political campaigner, she took care of the furnishings, planned parties and charity events, orchestrated the servants and instructed the children. A remarkable woman. After Hudson, Beryl was my favourite, she was the eldest child. Gerald was next, the oldest son who would become the second Viscount Devonport. Mark, the youngest, was the artist in the family and more prone to sickness than his siblings. The Kearleys stayed on Hiraethog for twenty-eight years and when they left, the lights went out in the main house.

During World War II, I was used for training the Home Guard. Before and after that, different gamekeepers lived here. Now another gamekeeper and his family are here. They have three children, two girls and one boy. Alis is the youngest. She talks to me and so I listen, but I don't always like what I hear from this family. They think I will fall apart. I say they are letting me crumble. Alis pulls bits off me and collects them in a tin box, which doesn't help and there isn't enough money for repairs. But perhaps I have complained too much about them. I don't want the lights and the fires to go out. As the snow settles on my roof, I feel its weight and I feel it sliding. More tiles will come off soon.

2

Alis

Alis knows that her older brother and sister are playing draughts upstairs, they will have seen the snow too, but won't go out for fear that their father will enlist their help with chores. He's fed the chickens and is bringing in peat bricks from the stack to burn in the grate. He always complains about the effort required to bring a dry peat brick to the fire: the digging, cutting, stacking, and carrying uses more energy than the brick will ever give—it's an old joke. Alis looks out and sees their father, their Tad, trudging towards the house. Already the snow is deep enough to hinder his progress. She runs down to greet him at the door. When he comes in he brings a wedge of cold air with him and she sees his eyebrows are frozen. He's ruddy-faced, with a dripping nose, his cheeks scaled with patches of greyish dry skin.

Alis opens her mouth to ask if he will take her out to play, maybe build a snowman, but sees his expression and changes her mind. Behind him, the doorway frames swirling snow before the door slams shut.

Supper is a broth with bread rolls that are soft inside. Alis takes the seat nearest the fire and removes her hat.

'It has hair,' says Dewi, her older brother.

She puts her hat back on and pulls her tongue out at him.

'Don't tease her, Dewi,' says their mother, removing the hat herself.

Alis reaches for her hat but her mother shakes her head and says: 'Leave it off while we eat, *del*.'

Mam carries the enamelled cooking pot to the table and they say grace before taking turns with the ladle. Tad goes first and Alis watches him through the steam that rises from the broth. She's pleased to see dumplings in there.

'When's moving day?' asks her sister, Gwen.

'It was going to be Wednesday, but now perhaps we'll stay until the road's clear,' their mother's shadow falls over the table as she stands up and reaches into the oven for more warm rolls. The first batch has gone, there's just one left that no one wants because it's cold.

Alis looks at her father. His fierceness subsides at the table and she can observe now, because he's oblivious when eating and won't feel the weight of her eyes on him. His eyebrows have thawed out, but the chapped skin on his cheeks remains. She wants to pick it off and wonders what he would do if she did. Shout and bleed? She watches his mouth move, full of bread and broth; juices dribble down his stubbled chin. She remembers the time that she and Gwen made fun of him, saying that his eyebrows looked greenish-coloured. There was a slippery moment when they thought he might be annoyed, but then he looked in the mirror and said: 'yes, they do look a bit green I suppose.' Alis remembers the relief; at least they hadn't pushed him too far that time.

She comes back to the present as she realises her brother Dewi is complaining about school.

'We gave presents. We got presents. Some people said: "glad you're leaving," we can't go back.'

'You have to go to school, del,' says their mother. 'It won't hurt you to go back for a few more days.'

'Can't we start the new school instead?' Dewi pleads.

'It's too far. You'll start there when we move.'

11

'If there's too much snow for moving, isn't there too much snow for school also?' asks Gwen, who can always be relied upon to jump to her brother's aid.

Alis watches, her eyes flitting from one family member to another. Their mother looks unsure. Alis guesses that their Mam just wants them at school and out of the way while she closes up their lives at Gwylfa.

'I don't want to move,' says Alis. She's checked her father's mood before throwing this morsel in.

Mam's frown deepens. 'We can't stay. Have you seen the state of the roof? This house is falling apart and anyway—it's sold.'

'Who is it sold to?' asks Alis.

'A local lady.'

'Are they going to fix the house?'

'Maybe. I think she bought it for the land though.'

'I want someone to fix it.'

'Well, they won't,' says Dewi, pulling his tongue out at his sister. 'It's all going to fall down, right on top of your head. Bang!'

'That's enough,' says Mam.

'It's not much more than fifty years old,' says Tad, his voice muffled by the bread he's chewing.

'Who built it?' asks Gwen.

'Ask your Mam,' says Tad, 'she did some reading about it.'

Gwen turns her attention to her mother, who has stood up to collect the dishes, but now sits down again.

'It was built by a millionaire, Hudson Kearley. Later he was a Viscount—.'

'What's a Viscount?'

'It's a name you give to someone important. It's quite a high rank.'

'Like a king or queen?'

'Not that high, a few levels below the king or queen in importance.'

'We don't like kings and queens though do we?' says Dewi.

'Don't we?' asks Mam.

'No, because they are English. My teacher always says the English are silly. He says, silly English making up rules like "i before e except after c" and then breaking their own rules.'

'Is that why you put stamps on the envelope upside down?' asks Gwen, looking at Tad. 'So the queen is standing on her head.'

Tad laughs and ruffles her hair.

'What were you going to tell us about the people?' asks Alis.

'I don't really know much,' says Mam. 'Just that we're living in a house that had lots of important visitors, but there aren't many records left to tell us what happened. Maybe they talked about government secrets here, who knows.'

'Lloyd George came here. He was the first Welsh Prime Minister,' says Tad. 'He was a good man, one of us.'

'There's a story that the Prince of Wales came too. They had lots of parties, although they didn't live here in the winter.'

'Was it empty in the winter?'

'No they had a caretaker to look after it, a bit like we are doing now.'

'If we go, who will look after the house?' asks Alis.

'Whoever has bought it will have to decide what to do,' says Mam.

Alis realises she won't be able to play at being a school teacher with her stuffed toys on the terrace anymore, nor can she pretend to be the princess that lives in the castle on the hill. She feels the beginning of something unpleasant stirring inside her. Like tummy ache. She puts her hat back on.

3

Beneath me runs the A543, opened in 1824 and once known as Ffordd Menyn (Butter Road) in artless times when dairies transported their goods that way, long before innocuous letter and number combinations became the convenient way to name a road. In those days, The Sportsman's Arms flourished as a posting house for horses and men. The road also brought in rich Englishmen with curled moustaches who began to picture high houses built on wholesome, health-giving moors and mountains. One such man was Hudson Ewbanke Kearley.

In my first incarnation, I was a huge wooden construct, bought at a trade fair in Oslo in the 1890s. While visiting Norway in 1894, Hudson became interested in Norwegian building techniques. In 1897 he bought The Sportsman's Arms and his purchase included an extensive parcel of land around the inn. This land rose to a high point on Bryn Trillyn, where I was later built. There was already a wooden chalet from Switzerland sited nearby, but it fell down one windy day.

They called me Plas Pren (wooden palace). I wasn't ugly as much as quirky. Bits were added on to the original structure, so that I looked more like a hamlet than a house. I was built in the wind by Norwegians in just a few days and the wind has been an enduring companion and assailant ever since. And it was not my only disparager, back then local protectionist voices were raised in disgust and the Free Press pounced upon the story.

'Why no Welsh builders?'

'Every bit of wood for Plas Pren was bought abroad.'

'Is this fair trade? Are we going to stand this?

'Foreigners who send in their manufactured goods like this should pay a fair share towards the income of this country.'

'Make them pay a one shilling tax on every £1. It would add thirty millions to our revenue.'

Wolfish winds hummed and drummed at my wooden shell and I leaked. An improved version also failed to remain water-tight. No tree stood on the top of Bryn Trillyn, no house built of trees would either. A third and final construction was undertaken, so determined was Hudson Kearley, by then a Baron, known as Lord Devonport.

Over the following decades, the Kearleys did much to assimilate themselves into local life, even when it was tedious for them. They raised money for charities, invited school children for tea on Bryn Trillyn, hosted suppers for shepherds at The Sportsman's Arms and sheepdog trials on the moors. Not all were impressed with their efforts and a well-known local misanthropist raised his voice at one shepherd's supper:

'It is a bribe all this, to keep us sweet. They don't care about us really. They have mansions and we have hovels. They build houses on our hills to look down on us.'

The gathering of almost fifty local farmers, shepherds, and gamekeepers at The Sportsman's Arms was quiet for a few moments as they considered these words. All knew that the Kearley family had paid for this dinner. It was an annual event around Christmastime and they were well-provided for in food and ale. The family did not attend since Christmas was spent at their other house in Buckinghamshire.

Someone made a noise, though most of the gathering could not be sure whether it was a word or a growl, but it sounded like assent. Another nodded in sympathy and still another spoke to break through the undecided fug that surrounded them:

'Let them build up there, they're welcome to the wind, rain, and snows...'

There followed a few noises of agreement and the mood of the room swung like a pendulum between hostility towards the absent family and some remembrance of loyalty and gratitude. Pipe smoke curled and coloured the room in a greyish veil and someone's spoon scraped their bowl.

'This is almost blasphemy,' cried a third. 'You are eating their food and drinking their beer. You complain about their goodwill because they are rich outsiders. And you do so under their roof and in their absence, when they cannot answer. But I ask would you not make the exact same complaint if they made *no* effort to befriend us? Would you say they don't care about us then also? Sit down and finish your food.'

This speaker was met with more noises and some spoken words that signalled agreement and within two minutes, raised tankards had collided in honour of the Kearleys. Rousing songs were sung, tables were thumped, and the stone floor resounded to stamping feet. From my vantage point on the moors I saw and heard. The misanthropist laid down his pitchfork and went home early.

Hudson helped fund a commemorative statue in Llansannan in attempt to show his commitment to the community. The idea came from his good friend and fellow Liberal MP, Thomas Ellis, who passed a month before its unveiling in 1899 and never saw it. With her ankles crossed as she sits, the cloaked girl statue is charming and looks pensive as she makes a garland of flowers. She leans upon a monolith that carries the names of five notable Welsh writers born in the parish of Llansannan. She is still there today.

4

Alis

'Let's play hide and seek,' says Alis as her mother clears away the dishes.

Dewi frowns. 'Boring.'

'In the other-house,' Alis adds putting her hat on.

'Well, it's cold there so you'll need the hat, especially if you're going in there alone. Do you know about the ghost?'

'There isn't a ghost.'

'There is,' says Gwen. 'Don't you know that the old man who lived here died of heartbreak after his son was killed in the war?'

'I don't believe you.'

'It's true. Tad said his son was a prisoner of war.'

'He came back,' says Alis. 'You can't scare me.'

'I meant the other son, the mad one,' says Gwen, twisting one of her blonde tresses around her finger, unable to hide the sly smile spreading across her face despite her efforts to look serious.

'Oh Gwen, you're a bad liar,' says Dewi.

'Anyway we can't get into the house, the door is stuck,' says Gwen.

'I opened it.'

'How? Dewi couldn't do it the other day.'

Alis giggles.

Dewi frowns, 'let's see if it's true.'

Wanting to be first, Alis rushes ahead, past their mother washing dishes, into the hallway and along it, all the way to the end, where it joins the other-house's hallway and there they see that the heavy door stands slightly ajar, just as Alis left it, except now there's little bits of snow on the tiled floor.

'I must've loosened it for her,' says Dewi, pushing at the door. 'Well, it won't move now. It's stuck and it's dark through there.'

He shoves it hard but Alis notices that he gives up quickly.

Gwen tries, but it looks like she doesn't really want it to budge either.

'Move,' says Alis, barging between them and shoving the door forcefully. It opens with a grinding of rusted hinge.

'The other-house likes me best,' she says.

They take one step into the dark side of the house, feeling its stillness. The walls exhale a musty dampness.

'I don't like it,' says Gwen, shuddering, 'it's like walking into a deep freeze and it's scary. Let's go back.'

Dewi hesitates for a moment and his light green eyes move from Gwen to Alis.

'Don't be such a baby crier,' he tells Gwen.

'We'll get torches,' he says, gesturing to himself and Alis, 'and you get a jumper so you won't whinge.'

Gwen wrinkles her freckled nose, but obeys.

With the torches, they can see into the library. Gwen stays behind Dewi. But Alis walks ahead. Their thin beams sweep over the books the Kearleys left behind, disintegrating on the shelves. Alis sees a beetle running along the shelf leaving trails in the dust. They are greeted by alarmed clucking as they point their torches at the shelves on the other side of the room. The chickens are roosting there.

'Sometimes I help Tad feed the chickens,' says Alis.

'I wonder if the Prince of Wales did come here,' says Gwen.

'The Prince of Wales is stupid anyway,' says Dewi. 'You know why he's called that?'

No one answers.

'It's so we know that England is in charge of us. They killed the real Welsh princes. Tad said Owain Glyndwr was the last of them.'

'Off with his head,' says Alis chopping her hand against the door.

A chicken flaps its wings, squawking.

'Don't scare the chickens,' says Gwen.

'It's snowing in here,' says Alis, pointing her torch towards the window where a tattered drape flaps and snow flies in through a broken pane.

The carpet squelches as they cross to the other door where the library joins the dining room, a larger room facing south with windows that look out onto the terrace. Their torch beams sweep the walls and someone illuminates a glaring portrait over an abandoned console.

'I've always wondered who that is,' says Gwen.

'Someone mean-looking,' replies Dewi, 'like a head teacher.'

'It's the lady of the house,' says Alis, reading the plaque beneath the portrait, 'Lady Sel-ina Dev-on-port. One of those people that used to live here.'

'You can read, that's good,' says Dewi.

Alis rolls her eyes at him. 'I've got a secret.'

'I bet it's something boring,' says Dewi.

'It's not. I found something in the other-house, but you can't tell Mam and Tad.'

'Why not?' asks Gwen.

20

'They'll take it away just like they took those special coins we found.'

'Well what is it?' asks Dewi waggling his torch impatiently and watching the effect of the light trails on the wall.

'We won't tell,' says Gwen. 'Promise.'

'Come on then,' says Alis. 'It's in the library.'

She leads them back through the door and approaches a pile of furniture, covered by a sheet.

'I put it under here for now, but I actually found it under the floor.'

'How did you get under the floor?' asks Dewi in a disgusted tone.

'Easy, there's a hole over there near the window and I shone my torch in it. And I saw this.'

She brings out a tin box.

'What's in it?' asks Gwen.

'Go on, open it and look,' says Alis. 'I'll hold it.'

Gwen swaps her torch to the other hand but then gives it to Dewi when she realises the rusted lid needs two hands to pry it open.

'Urghh,' she says, when it opens. 'What is it? Beetles?'

'No, no,' says Alis. 'Look properly.'

'It's jewellery,' says Dewi, shining both torches in. 'But it's all black. Looks like witch stuff.'

Gwen lifts out a black jewelled bracelet.

'Who would wear this?' she asks.

'A witch might,' says Dewi, as Gwen picks up a crescent-shaped item. 'Look at that, it's a black half-moon. I'm sure witches like moons.'

'That's a badge,' says Alis.

'You mean a brooch,' says Gwen, lifting out the final item. 'Oh look, a necklace and it has a locket on it. The locket is blue, not black.'

'Hmm, but the beads are black. Does it open?' asks Dewi.

'Not all lockets do. Oh but it does have a catch.'

'Let me do it,' says Alis as Gwen struggles. 'I found it.'

'No, I'm older so I'm better at opening things.'

'You're not better at opening doors.'

'Oh, I've done it.'

Gwen shrieks and drops the locket as something falls out.

'What was it?' asks Dewi, shining his torch on the floor.

'It looked like somebody's hair,' says Gwen, 'I thought for a second that it was a spider.'

'Look there!' says Alis and shines her torch. 'Is it moving?'

'Don't be silly,' says Dewi, picking up the lock of hair. 'It's not alive. Well, it's black.'

'Should we put it back in?' asks Gwen, still holding the locket.

'Yes we should,' says Alis.

'You do it then,' says Dewi handing her the hair.

'Oh it feels soft,' she says. 'Like Mam's.'

'I reckon that's more evidence of witches,' says Dewi. 'They use hair for black magic.'

'What do you know about that?' asks Gwen.

'Lots. They get a doll and put someone's hair on it and stick pins in it, and it really hurts the person if they do it right.'

'You're scaring me,' says Gwen. 'And I don't believe you. If you put hair in a locket it's from someone you love like your husband or wife or your child.'

'Nah. Witches, definitely,' argues Dewi. 'No one normal has black jewellery. I think we should show it to Mam.'

'No!' shouts Alis. 'They'll take it away. It's mine.'

'I agree with Alis,' says Gwen. 'We'll keep it for now. I'll wear the necklace and Alis can have the bracelet. You wear the moon.'

'I'm not wearing that,' says Dewi. 'It might have a curse on it.'

'Suit yourself,' says Gwen as she and Alis put theirs on.

'Don't we look lovely?' says Alis shining her torch on her wrist and then on Gwen.

'You look old-fashioned,' says Dewi.

Alis puts the box back and they return to the dining room and continue through the house.

The door at the far end is closed, like all the others. The handle is high for Alis but she turns it decisively and the door makes the usual protestations as it is pushed against its rusty hinges.

It opens into the hallway which leads to the front entrance of the house, now locked. Alis sees parquet flooring, coming loose in places as if an earthquake has hit the house; some pieces are missing altogether leaving dark rectangular holes.

'Don't step in the holes or you'll die,' she says.

'Baby stuff,' says Dewi purposely putting his foot into one, though Alis notices that he retracts it quickly and doesn't do it again.

As they are about to leave the front hallway, there's the sound of something falling.

'What was that?' asks Dewi, pointing his torch nervously towards the fireplace.

'The other-house is always making noises,' says Alis. 'It's falling apart you know. You two are easily scared.'

'Oh and you're so brave,' says Dewi sarcastically.

'Well, if you aren't scared, why don't you look up the chimney?' says Gwen, looking pointedly at Alis as she speaks.

'Yes good idea,' says Dewi. 'And you're just the right size to climb up it. Little children like you used to clean chimneys. Up you go.'

The hallway is cold, the wind moans under the front door and draughts move like ghosts. Alis shakes her head, but her older siblings block her exit.

*

'That's enough. We'll go upstairs,' Dewi decides.

Gwen hesitates on the bottom step as he begins to climb. The stair rods are rusted, the red carpet they once held, unravelling. It is snowing here too, flakes are drifting down the stairwell through a broken window and the wallpaper is hanging off. Alis pulls at the bits that droop—it's fun because they peel off easily. Dewi notices and grabs a large bit and pulls off a whole sheet, which falls in a wet lump onto the stairs.

'Stop it,' says Gwen. 'You're wrecking the house and it's not ours to wreck.'

Dewi pulls off another piece and looks round at Gwen, smiling in defiance, but she narrows her eyes and they move on, around the curve in the stairs and upwards. They have been in the bedrooms before, but not for a long while. When they first moved in, there was the tour of the house and both parents had regular jobs to keep the place looking nice, but recently there has been less to do and this is the first time they've been in here after dark. Alis has heard talk of money and when there's talk of money, it usually means there's not enough of it. Mam said the house was once fit for a princess, but it was a shame no one wanted it anymore. That had made Alis think of fairy stories and so she started playing the princess game. She used a curtain for a dress.

There are eleven bedrooms, but Alis has sneaked into the main house more often than her siblings and she knows where the best room is. She calls it the princess room because it's big and it looks out across the moor on the west side. It has gold and green drapes, a white and gold en-suite bathroom, and a dressing room with a big mirror.

'I'll show you the princess room,' she says turning the handle.

'That will be my room,' says Gwen. 'You're too filthy to be a princess.'

'I'm the oldest,' says Dewi, 'it should be mine.'

'Yes, you'd look good in a dress.'

'No, he'd be a prince,' says Alis.

'Princes are idiots. I'd be a knight actually,' says Dewi. 'Or if I must be a prince, I'll be Owain Glyndwr.'

The room is large and well-lit by the moon. Alis heads for the window seat. There's no furniture though so Dewi and Gwen quickly lose interest.

'Let's find a room for me,' says Gwen, who appears to have forgotten her fear. Dewi follows her out of the room, but Alis stays because she likes looking out at the snow. She's always liked the way the big cottony flakes fall, especially if you tip your head back, it's hypnotic. The room is freezing and feels damp, but the windows are intact here at least. She can hear Dewi and Gwen giggling and running along the landing. Outside the moor is brighter than usual with a waxing moon and the reflective pallor of the snow, but when she looks back into the room, she finds it more shadowy without the light of three torches and she can't hear the other two anymore. It's gone eerily quiet.

Alis rushes to the door and finds that it won't budge. She pushes against it hard and it moves a little but then pushes back against her as if someone is on the other side. Is it them? It's quiet for them. Normally they can't resist sniggering as they play their tricks. Desperate now, Alis throws herself on the door and whimpers, close to tears. Then Dewi laughs on the other side and when she pushes again she falls through.

'That was mean,' shouts Alis. 'You're always mean!'

'Oh, it was just a joke,' says Dewi, 'don't be a spoilsport.'

'I'm fed up of your jokes,' says Alis. 'I'm going back.'

'Don't go yet. Let's play hide and seek like you wanted,' says Gwen. 'You can choose whether to hide or seek.'

Alis spins the black bracelet round her wrist as she considers this and sees that Gwen's expression is contrite.

'Okay, I'll hide,' she says, thinking this is the safer option and because she knows a good place. There isn't much furniture up here, but there is a wooden chest in one of the rooms with nothing in it except for the curtain she uses as a dress.

'I'll hide too,' says Gwen and she beckons to Alis. 'No peeking, Dewi.'

Gwen tries to lead the way but Alis stops and turns to go the other way.

'Follow me.'

She takes Gwen round a bend in the corridor and into one of the bedrooms that looks south over the terrace. She shows Gwen the chest, but it's too tight for them both to get in and Dewi is speeding up his counting, probably because he's scared of being alone.

'I'll go in the next room,' says Gwen, sounding panicked.

With the lid shut, Alis lies in the chest with her torch on, but turns it off in case it's shining through the crack. It smells stale inside the chest. That old-fashioned oaky smell that the house has. There is a lot of wood in the house: fireplaces, wall panels, stairs, banisters and doors. Her father told her the house was once completely built of wood and that they built around the old shell, so it's all still there. Sometimes when there's a storm, it does feel like a ship at sea, creaking and groaning as the wind threatens to smash it to bits. She wonders where Gwen has gone, then she hears Dewi shout: 'found you!'

She waits for them to come for her and plays a game of turning her torch on and off until she becomes afraid of wasting the battery and stops. It is quiet again. She thinks she can hear small noises if she listens hard enough. It sounds like something is scratching at the window. A tree maybe? No. There aren't any trees up here. A bird then. She imagines it looks like some kind of pigeon. A queer night-time pigeon that scratches at windows.

The scratching stops and she turns on the torch and thinks this is what it's like to be inside a coffin. Except she's not dead. A creaking sound distracts her, like the sound of someone stepping on a loose floorboard. It sounds close. She holds her breath because she doesn't want whoever it is to hear her breathing and because she doesn't think it's Dewi or Gwen. Alis holds her breath for as long as she can then she releases with a gasp, which is noisy but she'd die otherwise.

Maybe whatever made the creak has gone. It looks like Dewi and Gwen have gone too. She turns her torch back on and feels angry tears forming. There is no excuse, Gwen knew her hiding place. She takes a deep breath and pushes on the lid of the chest. It goes up a little, but stops with an abrupt certainty. She tries again, but the same happens. Holding her breath, she remembers the little gold-coloured catch.

5

As the laughter of Gwen and Dewi dies away, I remember the other children who lived here. They loved to play hide and seek too, but not like this. Alis cries until she realises no one is listening. No one who matters anyway. After a while, when the moon has risen fully over the moor, her crying turns to an intermittent muffled sobbing. She has turned over, covered her face with her hands and given up on rattling the lid for now. No one has come to look for her.

A house makes all manner of noises. Now she is quiet, the girl may hear the delicate adjustments I must make, but she should not be afraid of creaks, taps and ticking noises. It is I, and not she, that is being assailed. My usual enemy is wind and rain, but let us not disregard the silent, gentle fall of snow. The romance of the white fluff belies the terrible weight of it. Alis may hear the grinding and grating of another tile slipping, but only I can feel it. She might also hear the scrape of mildewed curtain against a damp wall where a window is broken; a laboured squeaking where a badly-hung door is moved by draughts that pass, ill-humoured, along the passageway; or a mysterious knock on the main door. But the only spectres here are those of the past.

The child has started up again with her sobbing. There is a weary despair in her cries. Long ago another girl slept in this room. Not far from where that chest stands was a four-poster bed with purple drapes and next to it a sleek mahogany dresser. Beryl lay there one night in a dress the colour of forget-me-nots, with the curtains open and the lights off. She was unable to sleep. They all had a bit to drink that night. She did not care about how lovely the mahogany furniture or the violet and gold wallpaper was. She was looking at the stars and thinking about Lloyd George.

6

Hudson

8th August 1908

The journey from London to our summer home on the moors is the cause of much excitement. We have reserved a coach exclusively for ourselves on The Great Western from Paddington, but before we board the train, the railway bus carries us to the station. Our mound of luggage is secured on the roof rack, while we squeeze inside with our entourage of servants. At Chester we will be detached from the London train and shunted onto the Denbigh train.

As I stand watching on the station platform, three of a stack of five hat boxes have been opened as my wife Selina's new and rather inexperienced maid searches for the smart blue travelling hat that my wife prefers for train journeys. The other servants are busy transferring our luggage from the bus to the train, under my scrutiny. There will be no repeat of last year's incident where one of Beryl's dressing-bags was left behind at Paddington. I have left Selina to usher the children on, allowing her to deal with Mark, and his wheedling about having the whippet Nelly, with him. Beryl's beautiful gold-embellished harp is the last thing to go on. I am quite drawn to the thing. Its lines catch the eye like the musculature of a well-bred horse. I often run my hand over its outline and play a few bars when alone. Beryl is having lessons and has shown me. The harp has its own little story; it was the end result of a French holiday and an outing with Beryl in London. My close friend David Lloyd George had a say in it too.

It began with a holiday in Angers a few years ago when we happened to visit the Art Nouveau Café-concert de l'Alcazar on a night when the eccentric musical prodigy, Louis Vernassier was performing. The man could play a multitude of instruments and did so; these included a piano, xylophone, mandolin and saxophone, but it is the harp I remember. He performed dressed as a woman. I found myself focusing on the harp itself rather than looking at him. That was when I was first taken with the instrument. Whenever I did chance to look at Vernassier, I found to my embarrassment that he was looking right at me. I recall that I blushed rather forcefully.

Later, I repeated the tale to David Lloyd George, who I will call Dei for the sake of brevity. I remember him laughing loudly at my reticence in describing Vernassier and telling me that he would have enjoyed the spectacle. I have to say here that Dei enjoys living more dangerously than I do. Perhaps it has something to do with being Welsh. He also professed to a love of the harp and I must confess that the passions of my influential friend sometimes affect me.

Some weeks after, while on a shopping trip in London with my daughter, Beryl, we spotted a poster for Louis Vernassier and learned that he was bringing his act to the London music halls. Beryl wanted to see him again but I declined. In the same afternoon, by some coincidence, we were passing the window of a musical instrument shop when Beryl suddenly pulled away from me and pointed out a beautiful harp displayed alluringly in the window.

'Look!' she cried. 'It's like the one Louis Vernassier played. Oh I do wish I could have one.'

'Will you take lessons and practice hard?' I asked her.

'Yes, yes, I promise,' she cried jumping up and down inelegantly, so that I took her into the shop and bought the thing. I suppose there was the first sign that she would join a more artistic crew as she grew older. It is fitting that the harp should come now to Wales. As I board the train I can already picture it alongside the piano, with mother and daughter playing together. What parties we will host.

The train clatters out of the plains of the south towards the Black Country, where the sky darkens temporarily due to the chimneys belching smoke in this region, and then onwards we go towards the rolling green of Shrewsbury. Beyond there our eyes are drawn to the clouded twilight of Offa's Dyke; the rise in altitude brings about grander scenery with a wider palette of colour. My eyes are drawn to purple and brick red hills, an ancient barrier rising against the Saxons. Before I visited, I thought of Wales as a secret place of mists and sharp contours, where ancestors of the Celts lived in whitewashed cottages with slate roofs, shepherded flocks and spoke an alien tongue. Although Cardiff is cosmopolitan these days, on Hiraethog some might say I was not far wrong.

Our cook Mrs Findlay lays out a prepared lunch from a large picnic basket, on a folding table surrounded by sofas. We eat cold meats, bread rolls, cheeses and cake. It is an effort to speak for long against the clamour of the train so we settle into watching cities, towns and countryside rush by. It is cloudy and windy out, but from the safety of my seat, I am beginning to fully feel the return of my optimism, a low-key euphoria that has unexpectedly risen in me as I leave the bluster and histrionics of Parliament behind. There have been more vociferous debates than usual in the Commons this year. Our pensions bill has caused a storm. It is not the pensions as such but the requirement to pay for them. Churchill wants us to spend money on building the navy up as the Germans are building zealously. Dei is attentive to Winston's claims but more focused on getting the pensions through. I hope that when we reach Wales I can relax—I need a break.

Of course, Dei is going to fulfil his promise to speak at my house, so political debate won't be off the agenda completely. When is it ever? As soon as a man opens his mouth I find that politics of some sort comes spilling out, and that applies to womenfolk too. Nevertheless I'm looking forward to clean, clear air and abrasive winds that scour away all worries and cares.

I immerse myself with the rocking rhythm of the train. The boys are soon asleep but Beryl resists. She has finished her jigsaw and wants Selina and me to play bridge with her. The maids bring in afternoon tea and we play as the sun moves with us towards the west. I begin to succumb to sleepiness after losing the game.

*

I wake disorientated and see myself looking pale and surprised in the rattling, black windows. Everyone is asleep and a cold draught is blowing in. I regard the wan reflection of myself as if I do not know who this man is. It takes me a moment longer to work out that we are actually roaring through a tunnel and it is not yet dark at all. The murky threads of a dream hang about me, demanding to be remembered. For a few minutes I succumb.

I am approaching Gwylfa Hiraethog, admiring the new stone façade. The house is dominated by large windows that glint like eyes. I have often thought that houses have faces, though not always friendly. I think of Gwylfa's face as one that watches, with an impenetrable and indifferent wisdom. Perhaps this consciousness originates from Hiraethog and Bryn Trillyn; a land much older than the labels it bears. But back to my dream. I look up at the house as if I am approaching on the cart track to the frontal, east-facing elevation. The sky is rose-coloured, but I am not sure if it is sunset or dawn as the colour is not quite right. I look upon the house that has become dear to me and suddenly all the windows and doors open. Not by the hand of any person, but by themselves and all at exactly the same moment. It is uncanny and I am afraid, but I keep walking. Curtains are billowing out as if caught in a storm, although strangely it is not breezy and the air is quite still, heavy even. I realise then that the windows are smashed. All of them. As I watch, tiles begin to fall from the roof, which is becoming pitted with holes. The house looks shabbier, its walls are dirty, the paint is peeling, revealing dark, weather-beaten stone and brick beneath and this new blackness is stark, against the glowing sky. The walls appear less sturdy than I remember and holes are forming. Bricks fall from the chimneys, which are at the point of crumbling. In a moment I am sure a whole wall will collapse. I am transfixed in terror. The house is animated and demonic in the twilight. It disintegrates as if it has chosen to.

It is just a dream of course and these are the fancies of an anxious mind. I have left the cares of London behind, yet they are still swirling in my brain. Things have been organised at my London office and Wittington house is in the hands of my capable staff, but there are some issues up here. Although Gwylfa has been newly renovated I am concerned that it still retains some degree of ugliness, highlighted by the dream perhaps. I will speak to Sir Edwin Cooper about it. He has done a marvellous job in adding to Wittington House.

My organising brain is awake now and I brush away fragments of dreams. I take out my notebook and make a list of things to sort out. Tomorrow, I will meet with the staff to begin making arrangements for Lloyd George's visit.

We alight in Denbigh just after seven o'clock and although I am now eager to see that all is well at Gwylfa, my exhausted family want to eat supper as planned at The Crown Hotel. It is tradition. Denbigh is a medieval town built on a steep hill with a ruined castle at the top. The railway station is near the bottom of the hill and it is a steep climb up to The Crown Hotel, which is about halfway up. The car that has been sent for us toils with the gradient, even though it is a fairly recent model with a four-cylinder engine. It has a weather hood at least.

Mrs Hughes at The Crown Hotel is always welcoming. The table cloth looks new and she brings out her best crockery for us. Beryl loves the homemade rhubarb jam and I'm rather partial to eggs on toast. Selina just wants tea and cake. We end up with a hearty supper between us. The boys are groggy but plum pudding and tea will get them moving again.

'The Bull Hotel across the road is doing well,' says Selina as she pours my tea out. 'They have redecorated and I have heard it is looking very smart inside.'

'Fiddlesticks,' I say. 'It is a conservative establishment and we will not be setting foot in there. You can see enough of it through the windows. That will have to do.'

My wife raises her eyebrows at my terse reply, but chooses not to rile me further. She knows me well and often gets the better of me in debate, but is sensitive to my anxieties and the moods that occasionally take me. I know it is just the dream and being unsteady after the short sleep I had. She is a treasure who understands without needing to know all.

I favour The Crown Hotel because it is a friendly, Liberal establishment and the family that run it provide an excellent service. As if she can hear my thoughts, Mrs Hughes approaches our table with a smile.

'Is there anything else you need, sir?'

'Yes, a fair wind from the northeast to carry us up the mountain,' I say.

She laughs. 'I hear you have been made Baronet of Wittingham.'

'That is correct.'

'And I should address you as Sir Hudson Kearley and Lady Kearley now.' She claps her hands together with delight as she says this.

'You are always well-informed Mrs Hughes.' I smile, though her words have brought up a memory that is more likely to raise a frown. I didn't want the baronetage, a consolation prize for not making the cabinet, and I told Asquith as much. He wouldn't listen though; he said it would be a personal affront to him if I didn't take it.

'I like to keep up with Liberal politics, as you know, sir,' Mrs Hughes gives a funny little bow. 'What plans do you have for your stay?'

I am lost for a moment with the disagreeable memory and it takes me a few seconds to realise what she is asking.

'We do have something planned,' I say, at last. 'It is top secret at the moment, but as we are so well-acquainted, I will let you in on it.' I lower my voice and she leans towards me. 'We're expecting my good friend David Lloyd George later in the month.'

'The Chancellor of the Exchequer?' she asks.

'The very same.'

'Oh how wonderful! When?'

'He is in Germany on government business at the moment, so there is no exact date yet.'

'I must tell all my Liberal friends,' she says, then stops herself. 'When you say I am allowed to, of course. Until then, I can keep a secret.' She puts a finger on her lips.

'He has promised to do a public talk up at the house,' I say.

'Even better,' she cries, causing heads to turn as her customers begin to wonder what she is about. 'Keep me posted on the date.'

She is about to walk away when she remembers something.

'If I may be so bold, Sir Hudson, I hope that you will be able to visit us again when Mr Hughes is here, he has a clipping from *The Pembroke County Guardian* which he would like you to see. It's about how the Liberals and the Welsh have great hopes in Lloyd George and are dreaming of another Gladstone. It was written in April before he was even made Chancellor. A clever prediction we thought.'

I smile and decide not to tell her about the leaks concerning the cabinet reshuffle. The predictions made were not impressive given the number of people who spoke to the press. Dei himself was one of the accused. It wouldn't surprise me but I think it unfair to blame only him.

'We shall be back again before long and would be delighted to see the article,' I say, 'and do spread the news about the Chancellor visiting. I will probably get the papers involved, but there's nothing like the local network.'

After a little more excited chatter, Mrs Hughes leaves us to see to other, more neglected customers.

'You didn't need to tell her to spread the news,' says Selina, biting on the edge of a biscuit. 'Whatever you tell her gets into the papers every time we visit.'

I laugh. 'She is my Welsh publicity agent.'

I am ailing after the day's travelling and although I'm always pleased to hear of good reports from the capricious press, I think imagining Dei as a prime minister might be taking things a bit far. We have stayed longer than we should have, but at least we have a motor for the final leg of the journey. By carriage it was always a rather slow affair, although the old coaches had their merits; I confess I enjoyed the scenery more and they were rather romantic. Motors are convenient when they aren't breaking down, but they have a habit of scaring away all the wildlife that we used to enjoy watching.

The light is failing by the time we set off, driven by my chauffeur, Robert. We are heading towards Bylchau on a southwesterly, uphill route. The engine is noisy as we climb, but finally just after Bylchau, when most of the ascending is done, we come to open moor and a sense of height and space. Robert opens the throttle and we accelerate on the empty road, cool air rushing by so that we have to hold on to our hats. I am eager to see the house although I can't help remembering that confounded dream.

'I hope they've aired the place properly,' says Selina above the bluster. 'It was awfully dank in spring.'

'I expect they have,' I reply, having to shout to be heard. 'The damp issues should have been resolved with the building work.'

We pass the farms that are part of our estate, before roaring up a final steep hill with much chugging. After the summit we descend with a whoosh and take a bend around the dark, sparkling waters of Llyn Bran. Finally, we see the lights from our inn, The Sportsman's Arms. I won't call in now as I am eager to get to the house, but I'll take Selina down for lunch there tomorrow. Now we are beginning to ascend the cart track and the house will soon come into view over the hillside. The chimneys appear first, dark columns against the fading light, followed by the roof. I look for holes and then admonish myself for such absurdity. As we drive upwards, the house gradually reveals itself. From the front elevation, no upper windows are lit, but the lower lights are on to welcome us. I am looking forward to sitting in my favourite chair by the bookshelves with a reading light on the table next to me, a drink in my hand and the Welsh papers in my lap. Then I will know that our holiday has begun. The children are stirring now with some excited talk. When I say children, they are not so young anymore: Beryl is approaching twenty, Gerald is eighteen and Mark, is the only truly young one at thirteen.

Ahead of us the lit silhouette of the house looks well. There are no smashed panes as far as I can see in the dying light. No leaning chimneys or fallen tiles. They will tell me soon enough if there are problems, but tonight I want my comforts and already I feel freed by the expansive landscape falling to darkness around me; as if the cares and overcrowding of those cluttered plains far below are nothing to do with me.

7

29th August 1908

We have had three weeks of most enjoyable rest at Gwylfa and I am delighted to report that the house is in a good state of repair since the building works, although I confess there has not been much wind and rain to test it. Unfortunately, that is about to change as stormy weather is forecast. The timing is not good, but it has not prevented Dei's visit and our preparations are now complete. He and his wife Maggie are due to arrive in Denbigh at seven o'clock this evening and will be met by my chauffeur and a crowd of well-wishers. We will have a little party on Sunday night and on Monday Dei will speak to a local crowd here at the house.

It is morning now, Selina and the children are still upstairs but I'm out on the terrace. The sun is a weak presence and as is often the case here in the morning, it's misty and cool. The air is fresh though and despite the loss of my beloved views, I find that I enjoy looking into the swirling cloud. Ghosts. Life is full of them. Now that I've reached the great age of fifty two, I spend more time remembering than I used to. It's been a busy year for Dei, the year of his much publicised battles with the House of Lords, and with my help, he has brought in the Port of London Bill and also the Pensions Act. This is merely a break in the middle before it all resumes, but he will work through the break too. He has not long returned from Germany and after his visits in Wales, he will go to Scotland to meet Carnegie. His success as President of the Board of Trade has won him the admiration of many a doubter and when Sir Henry Campbell-Bannerman resigned with ailing health in April and Asquith stepped up to become the new Prime Minister, Lloyd George was offered the job of Chancellor. Dei wanted me with him as Financial Secretary to the Treasury, a role that I admit I am well-qualified for and would have been pleased to accept. Asquith would have given me the job but for some objections on the grounds that I have commercial interests in the City. Dei told me that I should mobilise my friends to coerce Asquith, but I refused. I wanted the job on merit and not through strong-arming the Prime Minister. Anyway, Asquith soon offered his apologies and said there would be a cabinet post for me in time.

I hope so because I have been feeling rather stifled in my old office. Winston Churchill got Dei's old job and I have to say it is much less agreeable now. Despite the successes and reorganisation of the preceding years, Churchill rather incongruously wants things to return to how they were before. I was secretly relieved when he lost his seat in Manchester and had to spend a lot of time out of the office in order to fight for the Dundee seat instead. While the suffragettes hounded him, I was left to do all the parliamentary work for the department, which suited me well.

I finish my coffee and turn to go in. Behind me the curtains billow out of an open window and I hear a piano being played. Handel's *Largo*. I find Beryl at the piano with Mark looking on. She stops playing when she sees me.

'You were told never to play that,' I say, barely controlling the anger that has risen in me quite unbidden.

'I'm sorry, Papa,' says Beryl. Mark says nothing, though I am annoyed to see him smirk.

'I will take that piece of music,' I say and without thinking about it I go over to the piano, snatch up the book and rip out the page that has *Largo* on it.

'But Papa, *Gavotte in C* is on the other side,' says Mark. 'We're allowed to play that.'

'Silence,' I say. 'You are being disrespectful! Did I not tell you that this was Mair's favourite piece to play for Mr Lloyd George?'

'It's only music,' mumbles Mark as he looks away. I am tempted to strike him, but I don't want any unpleasantness. It is only a matter of hours before the Lloyd Georges arrive and I want there to be a good atmosphere. I want them to see the remodelling work on the house and for it all to go well.

'I'm sorry,' says Beryl. 'It's my fault. I only wanted to see what it sounded like with it being so special to Mr Lloyd George. I would never have played it in his presence.'

'No. Well I am glad to hear that. Your apology is accepted,' I sigh, glad to release most of the anger that has overwhelmed me. 'Maybe you don't understand. His heart was broken when Mair died last November.'

'I understand,' says Beryl. 'She was very beautiful and Mama says she was his favourite child.'

'She was,' I agree. 'You must not mention her name at all.'

Beryl nods.

'What about if we want to talk about someone who has the same name?' asks Mark.

I decide not to be angry. I tell myself it is his age. He cannot help it.

'No! You will not talk about anyone with that name while they are here. Do you understand?'

He nods. I am glad to see the smirk has gone. They are good children really.

*

It is almost time; I haven't been able to settle today. The sun is low in the sky and I am sitting with Gerald in the library, half-heartedly reading the *Shipping Gazette,* when I hear shouting from above. It is Mark's voice. What mischief is that boy about now?

'The Chancellor's coming! I can see the motor!'

As I walk out into the hallway, Mark is sliding down the banister and Beryl shrieks and thunders downstairs as I hold up a hand to signal for calm.

'What have I told you?' I ask them.

Luckily, the servants are not so unruly and are ready at the door to greet our guests. The motor roars up the green cutting between the heather and round the final curve into the front driveway. I feel myself grinning as our friends wave and climb down. I allow my wife to embrace them first. Both look well and despite the tiring trip to Germany, Dei has lost none of his vitality.

It is important to me that he visits, since it was my Welsh friends, of which he is one, who inspired me to come here. I know that some of the local folk say my house is an ostentatious wooden shack, but it has been rebuilt with stone. I say let them come and stand in the shadow of this, my greatest folly, to hear my friend speak about things they should really care about. They may be glad of the shelter it provides.

Dei takes his wife's arm as they come into the house. Maggie now lives with Dei at 11 Downing Street, though she prefers Wales. I once heard him telling her, back in the early days, that he didn't like being left alone in London. He felt quite abandoned, but Maggie has always been strong. High society is not for her, nor is London the place to rear children. I think that's part of her charm for him, she has firm roots and although she takes great interest in Welsh politics, she is just not interested in Westminster or in being a society hostess. This has led to something of a fight amongst the eminent hostesses of London. In their opinion, if Margaret will not host parties for her husband, then they will, and now that he is Chancellor he is a sought-after guest. I'm not sure that all the flattery is good for the man and when Maggie is away, he is rather vulnerable to the attentions of all these ladies. I hope he isn't letting it all go to his head too much.

Dei is often labelled a socialist, non-conformist and radical, and though I share most of his beliefs, I do not resist moving in certain circles now that I'm a millionaire. He prefers self-made people, whereas I am not so discriminating. Of course, I am not deceiving myself either, there are some circles—usually guarded by stiffly-laced old matrons—that regard themselves as exclusive and that pour scorn onto 'new money'. They adhere to tradition and eschew change. I suppose they are afraid of what this supposedly radical government will do. I think they cling to the past in vain. And they never invite me or my wife to any of their parties.

After we have embraced and exchanged greetings, coats are taken and Maggie goes off arm in arm with Selina.

'Marvellous work on the house,' says Dei.

I update him on the changes we've made, while admitting that I'm still not satisfied.

'You're a determined fellow.'

His lilting accent is pleasing to hear, but I wonder if he is chafing me a little. The footman pours drinks and we step outside while we wait for dinner. We face east, looking towards Clocaenog Forest.

'Your house is renowned for height and views,' says Dei.

'The height was necessary for the views,' I say, feeling a need to defend my choice. 'Although I have heard from my gamekeeper that Gwylfa makes for quite a view for people to look up to.'

'I'm sure that is so. I cannot imagine that any lights have ever shone from windows on these dark summits before.'

His tone suggests a lack of approval, or am I reading too much into it?

'The wind can be fierce up here,' I admit. 'In fact we're in for a storm.'

'Is it habitable in the winter?'

'I don't suppose it would be unless good stores were kept in the cellars. I've heard reports of deep snow in these parts.'

We begin to walk the circumference. I often do this in the evening and it's become a ritual with visitors; always clockwise. We stop at the terrace on the southern elevation while I point out the Snowdonia mountain range, faint and hazy with distance and the Carneddau, north of that.

'And to the north is the coast,' I say. 'You can see the blue of the sea on a clear day, but the light is going now. Perhaps it will be clear enough tomorrow.'

'What do you intend for this house in the future, Hudson?'

I pause and find myself turning to look at Gwylfa as we walk past the north-facing side, which houses the staff quarters. I can see straight into the kitchen where the cook is preparing our dinner.

'It will go to the children equally. Gerald is my main heir of course. He will get the title.'

This is only the second time that it occurs to me that Gwylfa Hiraethog might be sold one day. The first time was when there was a storm and a heavy downpour during one of our parties. Several leaks started up that night and though a few of the guests tried to laugh it off, my pride was hurt and it occurred to me fleetingly to sell the wooden palace and to try

45

building in a sheltered valley somewhere else. It even occurred to me that I might buy a good house, already built and proven to be sturdy.

'How was your trip to Germany?' I ask, not liking where my thoughts are going. My words come out a little abruptly and I see him look sideways at me. I smile to let him know the little annoyance has passed.

He laughs as we continue to walk.

'It was no holiday at all, I was kept very busy. But if you have read the papers, you would think Churchill and I want to topple Sir Edward Grey and that my trip was designed to interfere with foreign policy and nothing more.'

'The press are always looking for an angle. It's nothing more than false propaganda, we know that,' I say.

'Yes but does the public know? Fling enough mud and some will stick. I rarely feel the need to justify myself but I have had to make some effort to counter these claims. As you know, I was there to look at the German systems for old-age, sickness and invalidity. I was impressed by what I saw there. It is very well-organised and fit for its purpose. I think that we should continue with our plans for a non-contributory pension scheme and consider a contributory scheme like they have in Germany, for invalidity and sickness. But before I can make a definite decision, I need to visit Belgium and Austria to investigate their schemes.'

'It does appear that many European countries are ahead of us in this respect.'

'I agree. We have learned this year in particular of how archaic some aspects of British politics are. There is much unrest and I fear we cannot ignore the worker's unions, the suffragettes, and the Irish question. If the government does not act, or if other powers prevent the government from acting, I do think we could eventually face some sort of revolution.'

I nod. I have thought this myself at times.

'How are relations with the Germans?' I ask.

He looks across at me and then smiles.

'Well, off the record we *were* there for another reason.'

'Oh?'

'I made them an offer.'

'What offer?'

'I pledged a slowing in naval expansion in return for the same on their side, but they rather took offence. As you know we need money for our social reforms and who needs militaristic expansion in peacetime? It's downright wasteful. There are better things for us to spend on.'

'What did they say?'

'They refused. Our offer wasn't meant as an insult, but to them it was.'

'But relations are still good?'

'Were they ever really that good? On the surface it all seems alright. I don't understand the German language, but I do understand men. I realised on that trip that we make the mistake of thinking that others share our perception of things, when they don't.'

'The Prussians are a military people.'

'Yes and we are in the way of their plans.'

'Did you meet the Kaiser?'

'No. I was promised the Kaiser but I got Vice-Chancellor von Bethamnn-Hollweg instead. I can't even remember the excuse they gave. The Vice-Chancellor was good about showing me their social insurance schemes. He was a nice chap until we attended a meal supposedly in my honour. At Berlin Zoo in the great hall. Champagne to start, followed by beer. Von Bethamnn-Hollweg had too much of both if you ask me. Then he lost all restraint. He got rather vehement about what he felt was Britain's encirclement of Germany. A few others joined him. There wasn't a passivist in the house. I was glad to leave in one piece.'

'Oh, I say. It doesn't sound good. I've often thought we need some sort of peace agreement in Europe. What is the forecast there?'

'I was left shaken up a bit, I will not lie. But I don't yet believe it'll come to war. I still hope that good sense will prevail. We all shook hands in the end of course but I've had to change my view somewhat. We will have to keep building the navy. I've got a sense of what the Prussians want now.'

'Oh?'

'They couldn't hide it or didn't care to. They are eager for power and influence in the world and they want their day in the sun. Britain has an empire so why not Germany? I don't think they care about the consequences. Our control of the seas is an annoyance. I was left with rather a sinking feeling.'

He sighs.

I am feeling a bit unsettled by his words when he suddenly stops walking and looks across the moors with glistening eyes.

'Are you well?' I ask.

'I am, Hudson. That's just it. I am frightfully happy to be back in the homeland.'

8

30th August 1908

I hear the civilised clatter of glasses as the footman pushes the drinks trolley over the threshold into the drawing room. Beyond mullioned windows, the blue sky is tracked with cloud, but it is the purple of the heather that always takes my eye at this time of year. The weather is often good in August, but the storm is due tomorrow.

'You can close the windows now,' my wife instructs the footman. 'It's getting rather chilly.'

Evening is upon us again. This morning we attended a service at Pen-y-Cefn chapel with Dei and Maggie. He chooses non-conformist places of worship and is a strong advocate for reform and disestablishment in Wales. After his weekend here, he will go on with his wife to the palace in St Asaph for a stay with the Bishop. It will be an interesting visit I'm sure for the Bishop is a supporter of the Church of England and though they have become friends in recent times, they have been adversaries for longer.

Now we are in the drawing room after a fine meal. Dei sits holding a small glass of whisky as we talk politics. I've noticed how his eyes follow my daughter. The man has a reputation as a philanderer, but I think I see only sadness as I watch him watching her. She's not much older than his daughter Mair would have been, had she survived.

I try to distract him.

'Home Rule for the Irish will open the flood gates,' I say. 'The Welsh and Scottish will want the same.'

Dei turns to me and I'm aware of the steel of his eyes as he regards me.

'Or it might close the gates for good,' he says.

'How so?'

'Once the campaigning power of the Irish National Party leaves parliament, the Welsh will be weak.'

'You are often right where others are wrong,' I say. 'But I don't believe we'll get Irish Home Rule past that prehistoric legion of peers. They veto at Balfour's command.'

I underline this point by throwing back the last of my whisky.

Dei is silent for a while and I'm pleased by that. But just as I dare to think that I've got him, he bangs his glass down on the table and laughs.

'There must be a limit to the unelected impeding the march of progress, Hudson. If the Lords continue to veto policies that they do not like, then perhaps the time has come to veto them.'

He winks and I laugh.

'How can we veto them?'

'Reduce their powers.'

'Indeed, but how exactly?'

'It will have to be something big. Something that the electorate really care about.'

'Do you have something in mind?'

'It may already be happening.'

'The pensions,' I say and he smiles.

'If social reform can be packaged financially, they can't interfere.'

'When you're Prime Minister?'

'You think a radical like Lloyd George will ever be Prime Minister? More than half the cabinet and all the Whigs are against me,' he laughs, but I see a spark in his eyes and I wonder.

'You're in position for such a manoeuvre. Who'd have thought a few years ago that you would be appointed Chancellor?'

'Yes and as Chancellor, there is much I can do to agitate the peers if they choose to become too much of an obstacle. The budget may yet be the staff that forces the gates of hell open and lets the furies loose.'

Perhaps I've had a few too many drinks because my waistcoat feels tight and I'm laughing too much. Often when I'm sitting and talking politics with Dei, I have the feeling that I'm in the shadow of a greatness that I can't articulate. I want to say that he's a force of nature and almost open my mouth to speak, or perhaps I could tell him he is the uncrowned king of Wales, or that I fear the Tories would rather like him to defect to them as Gladstone did. But I stop myself for fear of becoming a red-faced buffoon. Some things are difficult to say as well as they are felt, and I am known as a great organiser, not a speaker. Even so, he talks to me as an equal as I dance about a cliff edge, sometimes hanging on by my fingertips, sometimes falling off, or slipping at the verge. I dance a jig inside when I say something that makes him stop and think. And even though I should feel secure in this moment as we sit nursing our whisky, I feel that he is slipping away from me; already I look back fondly on our past. I'm thinking of our days on the Board of Trade when I was his secretary and confidant. I remember laughing at his jibes about the Tories when they lost every seat in Wales in 1906 and how the Lords were nothing more than Balfour's poodles. There was much laughter and cheering when he spoke of that in the Commons.

After we have imbibed a little more, we stop caring about politics and Gerald puts the gramophone on.

'Not Debussy,' says Selina. 'An ugly creature with deplorable morals. Something else please!'

Gerald doesn't argue and replaces it with some jolly band music. My wife must be drunk and I wish she hadn't spoken thus; it is not like her at all, and Debussy did marry in the end. Selina is usually a most gracious and kind lady, but not everyone has the same high morals and I do not want it to be awkward for Dei. Luck is with us because the moment passes quickly enough and Beryl gets up to dance the polka with Gerald. Dei joins them soon after, coercing Maggie who reluctantly acquiesces but is soon laughing, and I smile across at Selina, who rises without a word.

Later we dance the waltz to Strauss, and I take a turn with Maggie and then Beryl. I am uncomfortable during my dance with Maggie because I am watching Dei dancing with my daughter. Beryl has been resistant so far to the men she has met since her coming-out and I worry about her in a way I do not have to with the boys. I will be relieved when she finds a deserving young man. She has a rather unsettling habit of talking to the male servants too. I have even caught her talking in a rather inappropriate manner to a certain young Welshman who works here. When I admonished the boy, he said nothing, but his father later told me that it is Beryl who seeks him out. I wanted the boy dismissed, but Selina thought that would be unfair and we spoke to Beryl instead. She denied it all of course. Now she is whirling about on Dei's arm, with a blush to her cheeks and shining eyes. I try not to watch too much as Maggie has noticed and it is rude and unfair to her, but my eyes keep drifting. I suppose Dei always looks like he is flirting, even when he is not. The man has an energy that few other chaps have; he is not easily contained. With his chiselled cheekbones and that sparkle in his eye, I suppose no woman can resist. Poor Maggie is not smiling anymore. I think she wants this number to be over, as I do. The Blue Danube is my signal to take my daughter back from Dei. She looks lovely tonight in a blue dress with a net of jewels sparkling in her dark hair. Her eyes are shining. I hope it is not because of Dei. He is dancing with my wife now and I observe that she also is smiling a little too much for my liking.

'Papa, why are you frowning so?' asks Beryl.

'Am I? Oh, I'm sorry. It seems that it is not easy to leave London behind.'

'You work too much,' she says.

I smile and make an effort to relax. I will speak to Selina soon about having a party when we return to Wittington. I'm sure we can find some marriageable young men for Beryl.

*

We retire at midnight after Dei has beaten me and the boys at chess. Only Beryl was able to unhorse him and he denies that he let her win. Although I think it is probably harmless, the coquetry between them as they played was unnerving for me. I glanced at my wife a few times to see if she had noticed but although she and Maggie were both sitting nearby and partially observing the spectacle, they did not appear uneasy. Is he flirting with our nineteen-year-old daughter, or am I just misreading the situation? I sit on my bed and look into the amber liquid in my glass as if to find the answer there. Perhaps that is the answer; I have drunk too much.

I hope that he is comfortable. He is in the largest of the south-facing guest rooms. In the morning he will wake to coffee, a cooked breakfast and views of Mynydd Hiraethog. If it is clear he'll be able to see the mountains. I look forward to hearing if he is impressed.

'I'm worried about the weather forecast,' says Selina.

I watch her maid combing out her hair. I think it rather amusing the way it sticks out like a letter M when she removes all the pins and the pompadour frame.

'Yes, he would have been better doing his speech today,' I say, 'but he was not worried when I told him. He is a Welshman after all; he's used to it.'

'Maybe,' says Selina, 'but he lives in a valley and we are exposed on a mountain.'

'Why do you think I chose this spot?'

When she has climbed into bed and lain down next to me, I pull her close and put my arms around her. The silk of her nightdress is cool, but her warmth diffuses into me and I rest my head against her, grateful for the roundness and sturdiness of her shape and the solidity of another body to ground me.

'If there is anyone who can speak into a storm, it is David Lloyd George.'

'But who will come here in this awful weather?' she asks.

'They will come.'

9

31st August 1908

He is on the balcony and his hair stands up in the wind so that he looks rather mad. I am nervous about opening for him. In spite of the inclement weather, Selina's fears were unfounded and a crowd has gathered on Bryn Trillyn to hear his speech. There is little shelter, but these people are accustomed to howling wind and lashing rain. They have come to see a Welsh Chancellor of the Exchequer speaking on a Welsh mountain. I fear this will never happen again in my lifetime and some emotion stirs me as I open for him, shouting into the churning air:

'Please welcome my close friend David Lloyd George, a man whom I have had the privilege to work with as the Secretary to the Board of Trade during his presidency there. David is a man who gets things done, a man of great principle and action. And this storm today will not prevent him from speaking any more than the storm the Tories raise in the House of Commons!'

There is applause, whistles and shouts and Dei steps forward. He raises a hand to wave and waits for the crowd to fall silent.

'I am very pleased to see so many of my fellow countrymen here on Mynydd Hiraethog.'

The wind howls around the obstruction that is my house, but Dei raises his voice to match the wind.

'I do not know if I will be blown away by this storm now that I am here. I have observed you walking up the mountain and I see the might of the Welsh. The storm has raged, the rain is beating hard, but in spite of this, Wales is climbing to the fore. The rich pluck food from the mouths of the poor, but now there is a Welshman in government and he will ensure that Wales will not be forgotten.'

Below, I see shining upturned faces washed by rain, and hands holding onto hats. Some may be here to see one of their own risen to greatness, others because they've heard that Dei is a skilful speaker. I hope they also know about the reforms he is fighting for.

'You people live in the heart of a mountain, while I come from Criccieth, a picturesque seaside town, although still too, amongst the hills. I remember well of how I used to walk to school each morning and although I lived in a vale, I had to cross a hill on my way. And it gave me a wonderful view of the mountains and implanted in me a remarkable spirit of enthusiasm with which to face my work of the day. The mountains, to me, have a certain enduring power, and the power of these mountains has taken hold of the life of Wales. We are living in historical villages, with many stories in their past. Stories that I hope will not be lost. Do you ever read the history of your own country?'

He pauses to hear their answers. A few shake their heads while some look around to see what others are saying. A young woman shouts 'no,' into the pummelling wind.

Lloyd George nods, acknowledging her answer. 'When I was in school, they taught only the history of England, as if our Welsh history was not worth knowing. I knew of England's kings and queens, the dates of their births and deaths, but was not taught the history of Wales. That has made me sad.'

Voices rise in agreement.

'Here you are, living on Hiraethog amongst the graves of your predecessors. But what do you know of them? Henry I's soldiers were seen here in this neighbourhood, when Owain Gwynedd challenged the tyrant. And on that occasion the English were defeated and driven out, thanks to a great Welsh prince and the great Welsh weather!'

People cheer at that.

'After that, the tyrant went away and there was peace for a time. This country has raised valiant men such as Tudur Aled, Henry Rees and Gwilym Hiraethog. A hundred years hence the names of these men will be treasured as they are today, such is their greatness.'

The wind is strong, but Dei stands firm and it carries his words for him. He shouts, even louder than he does in the Commons, and I can't help but notice that between gusts, when the wind goes quiet, his voice drops too.

'If we are not proud of our heroes of the past, it is time we should be. And what about the English? They have the Plantagenets, the Stuarts and the Tudors, but they have all departed while Hiraethog is still here, with its language and customs intact. The authorities have tried to make Englishmen of us, but in spite of being forced to attend Anglicised schools and churches, we are more Welsh than ever.'

The crowd are with him now. Cheers rise and are thrown down the hillside by a brilliant gust. I imagine his words and their cries carried and freed to fly across the moors like small birds surfing on the wind. Perhaps some vowels and consonants will reach as far as Llansannan or even Denbigh, and those who didn't come will hear a small part of Dei's speech. And maybe they will wish they had come.

'It is our duty to kindly point out our faults to one another and to take part in healthy debate, always remembering that we are one nation. But we should not point out our faults to strangers, for they will not understand. We are a flood rising, a small nation ascending while the powers at the top try to beat us down, but we won't be broken. We are tough and resilient. We have to be, with weather like this!'

The crowd laughs and huddles together as a new wave of rain comes across in sheets, as if to prove his point.

'In conflict we are made strong. Do you know, I rather enjoy reading newspapers that are against me? I was in the workshop that is the Board of Trade with my good friend Hudson Kearley here, but now I am the chief publican. They refer to me as if I were nothing more than a rate collector. They cannot understand how a Welshman, and quite a radical one at that, could be Chancellor of the Exchequer. No one cares too much for the man who makes up the taxes. Some of them have never seen a Welshman and have the strangest ideas about us!'

'And if I campaign for Welsh issues, I get called a Welsh thief! They will never be happy with having a sharp-tongued dragon on the Treasury bench. But I have made up my mind to be fair to everybody and for this reason my opponents have been surprised.'

As his voice drops, Beryl comes to my side and links her arm through mine. I notice that she is as soaked as I am. Her hat droops and tendrils of hair stick to her face. The boys are watching from an open window, while my wife has already withdrawn, not wanting to appear dishevelled in front of a crowd.

'I am a child of the people. One of you. I was brought up among you in Wales and I know of your trials and tribulations.'

His voice rises again now and the tempo picks up.

'And I wish to add nothing further to the anxieties of your lives but instead to do something to lighten your load, which you have borne stoically, with such fortitude. It is my plan to carry out long-desired and long-promised plans of social reform; to that end, the Pensions Act will bring relief to a million men and women in their declining years.'

He pauses as the crowd cheers, the loudest cheer so far.

'Of course the Tories and their cronies in the House of Lords set to crying whenever we try to push some reform through. And I ask you to consider the Upper House and what it is exactly. A selfish and irresponsible assembly wilfully causing a senseless obstruction to the path of progress. We have been voted in by the people, yet they veto the policies you voted for and refuse to let us govern!'

Some jeering here, anger at those obstructing Lords, I presume. His voice is strident, then soft.

'And I asked the Tories, if they are so opposed to the Pensions Act, then why do they promise to introduce it themselves every time they stand for election?'

Laughter, and boos.

'They said they were worried about the common man who has to pay for these pensions,' his voice has dropped now and he pauses for effect.

'I told them that this was a worry we shared. I put it to them that perhaps the common man shouldn't have to pay anything and that those who are better off can foot the bill. After that I'm afraid they drowned me out with their wailing.'

Further laughter and some anger. More people have arrived since the start and the crowd has swollen. Another squall rises but Dei does not wait for it to abate, he uses it to carry the final words of his speech:

'No more of the workhouse for men and women over seventy. The pension of five shillings a week will ensure that the old will no longer be destitute; they will not have to labour in old age as they have all their life, without the adequate rest and recreation that is needed by the human spirit. And they will no longer have to live in penury in their final days. It is the duty of all of us, the government and the well-off especially, to ensure that we do not unfairly profit from thousands of hardworking men and women living lives of ceaseless toil. We must make adequate provision against the scourge of poverty!'

After enthusiastic applause, a man shouts out something about Home Rule just as the Bishop of St Asaph arrives.

'I admire the unity of the Welsh people and the fact is that we agree on things as a nation. I can confidently say that we do not have an Ulster and because of this any Welsh claim for Home Rule has more legitimacy in many ways than Ireland. That is not a criticism of the Irish position, merely a fact. However, the campaigning power of the Irish National Party should be an inspiration to us here. I am a supporter of Home Rule for Wales too, that I have made clear.'

'What is being done about the Church of England?' shouts a woman. 'Have you forgotten about that since you've become Chancellor?'

I glance towards the Bishop who is standing with his retinue at the back.

'I support disestablishment as many here will know,' says Dei. 'I have prioritised education reform in Wales because education is controlled by the church, and I will continue to campaign on all fronts for religious freedom in Wales and for an end to paying taxes to benefit English landowners and clergy. I thank you all for enduring the storm here today to hear me speak and am humbled by your applause. Long live Hiraethog!'

I wonder what the Bishop thought of that. It will certainly be the ignoble elephant in the room during the visit to St Asaph. But what's this? Lloyd George is asking the Bishop to come up and address the crowd and the Bishop has just refused. I realise I am holding my breath. The Bishop is shaking his head, but nevertheless all is well, the Reverend Robert Williams is going to speak and then Colonel Wynne will make his address; we are saved.

*

We say our goodbyes to Dei and Maggie as the crowd leaves the mountain and the Bishop's brougham waits to take them away. The wind has dropped and I am praising Dei for his speech as he embraces me firmly.

'Give my best to Winston and good luck with the Bishop,' I say.

'No need to worry there. He and I have been on good terms since—' He suddenly looks crestfallen.

I pat him on the shoulder.

He is rather subdued for a moment, but then rallies, 'I will see you tomorrow at the Eisteddfod, old fellow,' he says, taking me by the shoulder and giving me a shake. 'Winston may come too.'

There is laughter dancing in his eyes and I amazed at his recovery. I realise I must look a bit glum, so I force a smile as I watch them go. It has started to rain again.

10

I am reminded of a holiday in France with Dei. It was not long after his triumph in the railway dispute when I was impressed by how he brought each side together to mediate; this was not normal practice at the time. However, he did not have long to enjoy his success due to the grave tragedy of his daughter's sudden death from appendicitis. I encouraged him to take a holiday after his secretary found him asleep in the office and worried about what he might do if left alone. Dei had thrown himself back into his work and had become dangerously exhausted. He was utterly demented with grief and spoke of 'some hand from the dark' that had taken Mair from him. It is true that Mair was his favourite. It would have been hard not to love such a beautiful and gentle soul as she was, but Dei did appear to prefer his daughters. I try not to have favourites myself, but from time to time one can be more beloved to me than the others. I will say no more on it.

A holiday was also suggested by the Bishop of St Asaph. I never saw the letter, but it touched Dei. Even though they had been adversaries, the Bishop had reached out because he too had lost a child. Dei asked him to come with us to France, but the Bishop was unable. The holiday turned out to be a useful distraction, but it was not without incident.

I decided on a motoring tour down to the French Riviera. We were both fond of motoring in those days. We set out on 20th December 1907 with my boy Mark and Dei's sons, Dick and Gwilym, in my Napier. The youngsters helped keep our spirits high. In his grief Dei was glad to be missing a Christmas at home in Criccieth. In addition, Lady Nunburnholme had most kindly put her charming villa La Pastorelle—located in a quiet part of Nice—at our disposal. This is where we intended to spend our Christmas, although in the end we didn't get there until 4pm on Christmas Day.

I took charge of the driving in order to allow Dei some relaxation. We stayed in Boulogne on our first night and after that in Meaux and Lyon. On Christmas Eve we left Lyon for Aix-en-Provence. Lyon was a somewhat confusing place to leave despite the directions I had specifically asked for at the hotel. We started out early in the morning in order to make good time, but it was still not fully light, and drizzle with dark clouds did not help visibility. We were told to cross the river over the Pont des Chataigniers, the last bridge on the quays. However on reaching the bridge, Dei insisted it was not the last bridge and that there was another bridge, and that we should continue. I started to argue but he was insistent and I did not want to upset a grieving man. It turned out to be just a railway bridge and so I turned around and put my foot down in order to return to the correct bridge more quickly. I was doing a good thirty miles an hour when out of nowhere an enormous hay wagon loomed up before us. Most unexpectedly, the car went into a sudden and violent skid. I am unsure to this day as to what caused the car to shoot towards the hay wagon. I think it must have been the wet weather and the slippery tram-lines. I am not sure what I did, but I think it may have involved some quick action with the steering wheel and brakes. The terrified look of the boy in charge of the horses and wagon is forever imprinted on me. We skidded again as a result of my manoeuvring, but avoided a crash and got away safely in the end.

'That was very well done,' said Dei, who was sitting in the box seat next to me.

Later, after we had crossed the bridge and fully recovered from the ordeal, praise turned into blame.

'You were angry,' he said, 'you were angry because I made you pass the right bridge.'

I think I frowned at him, but did not reply.

'You were angry,' he repeated, 'that's why you drove faster and that's what caused it.'

I am used to his teasing ways although on this occasion I wanted to tell him that his poor directions had gone some way towards causing the incident, but I held my tongue.

'If you say so,' I said quietly.

Of course Dei was right. I had accelerated the motor in annoyance at the delay.

We reached Aix-en-Provence safely and spent Christmas morning there, before setting off for the villa in Nice. Dei and I talked politics as always and it was then that we predicted that he would become Chancellor. Campbell-Bannerman had suffered a serious heart attack and his health was failing. We knew he would be forced to retire before long.

'He's a dead man,' I said, 'at least politically.'

Little did I know then, that Campbell-Bannerman would actually be dead within a few short months.

'Who do you think will succeed him?'

'Asquith, of course,' I replied, surprised that he should ask.

He nodded. 'Yes quite, yes, I quite agree.'

Yet something in his manner told me that he didn't think Asquith was the man for the job and my mind returned to a secret meeting I'd witnessed between him and Morley.

'Where do you think he'll put you?' I asked.

He shrugged, 'I don't know. What do you think?'

'Chancellor of the Exchequer,' I said, watching him closely.

'I should like that,' he said with more innocence than I believed was genuine. 'But why do you think that?'

'Asquith will not leave you on his flank. However, something might ruin your chance.'

He looked over at me then. 'What would that be?' he asked.

I detected a hint of unease in his voice. 'You being involved in an intrigue,' I said and watched him blush in response to this. It was a rare thing to see him embarrassed like that.

'What is Morley up to?' I asked.

He looked down resignedly and then proceeded to tell me all about it. He admitted that there was already some attempt afoot to oust Asquith from succession to Prime Minister. Dei played down his involvement. I don't think it mattered in the end. The scheming of a few men was not enough to alter Asquith's course.

We did quite a bit of socialising on that holiday. Our dinner with Lord Glantawe gave Dei some comfort as here was a man who had lost five children and somehow survived. Dei also enjoyed the company of the Henrys, Charles Henry was a millionaire merchant and Liberal MP and I think Dei was rather drawn to his wife Julia who was tall, dark and attractive. They were later rumoured to have had an affair from which he had trouble extricating himself, but on that occasion, Dei was still close to Maggie and during our holiday he wrote several letters to her. In fact, poor Mair's death had brought them together; at least for a while.

11

Beryl

I could not sleep the night I beat Lloyd George at chess. I lay on my bed, with the curtains open and looked out at the moon shining over the moor. I waited for him, but knew he wouldn't come.

I came out in London and attended many balls and parties. Even here in Wales, my Mama and Papa have put events on to help me meet suitors, and I did everything I was told. There were less young men in Wales though, and the ones that caught my eye were taken. I felt on the edge of things always, even though I was not particularly shy. In my mind I see circles joining together in figures of eight and expanding to create concentric patterns, and I'm always skating round the edge somehow and never quite able to reach the middle, where I imagine that things will be happening. Sometimes, I look back and think of missed opportunities, that I had a chance but I was like a blinkered cart horse trudging forward and missing everything to the right and left. And now even though I am only nineteen, I appear to have settled into a kind of fatalism; beliefs that I'll never marry or have children have grown in me like weeds, and I just cannot seem to go beyond that.

This is how I find myself behaving in a reckless manner. Even at parties full of old, married men I engage in pointless flirtation, much to the disapproval of my father. That night I disgraced myself with Lloyd George over a game of chess, I saw and felt my father's eyes on me, yet I continued. Lloyd

George is in his forties and his wife was in the same room, but there is something about the man. He has risen fast, even though he came from a poor beginning, and he's Welsh. Yet it is not hard to believe in his success, when you see the passionate energy and beauty about him that makes you want to get close; as if he's a font of nectar to drink from. He is so alive, and our house reverberates with his presence. It's intoxicating for me that he gave me much of his attention during the visit. Perhaps he only likes me in a confused way because his daughter Mair died. I think of Mair and am ashamed, but still some wickedness has stirred in me. Maybe it was the wine they let me drink.

I am still restless even after we have waved off Mr and Mrs Lloyd George, and I go looking for the boy servant that I have been watching for a while. No longer blinkered, no longer moving on the edge of circles, I go straight to the kennels where he is washing my father's car. He barely makes eye contact, though he sees my approach. He has been told not to talk to me. I stop and stare and he looks behind to see if there is someone there to warrant my attention. When he realises it's him I look at, he ignores me and continues to wash the car, except now I see the colour rise into his cheeks. He is a very pretty looking man, though I have mostly only seen him in profile as he avoids looking at me. He knows his place too well, and maybe he is shy too. His hair is overly long on top, but I like the wild way that it curls, and his fringe falls in the way of his eyes, I see his lashes are long enough to make a girl proud. He is of a medium height and slim with muscular arms. I think of rejected suitors with flabby faces and flaccid bodies and wish for one like him with his level of humility. Anyone who came close to this level of physical beauty in my society would carry himself with arrogance and look upon me as not beautiful enough. This boy's quietude inspires and intrigues me.

After I have gazed upon him, I leave the poor boy alone but not without one last look back as I walk away. He is observing me through his fringe but looks down quickly when he sees that I am staring again. It is so unladylike of me but where has being good got me? I wish for a camera to take a picture of him, but I have to make do with remembering. As I walk back to the house I look up at the shiny glass of the windows and see only sky and scudding clouds reflected. I hope that my parents and brothers haven't seen.

12

November 1908

The shooting is over and the Kearleys have returned to the other house, Wittington. I am glad of the quiet after the guns. The decimated bird life can come out of hiding and begin to recuperate.

If you listen, it is never silent here; even a gentle breeze has its music, and there is often some bird cry or song. In the summer, skylarks sing ecstatically as they fly in vertical lines. There are also curlews, their curved beaks and long thin legs are those of the coastal wader, but their exotic babbling is welcome as they return to nest here every year. At other times buzzards mew as they soar far above in circles on broad mottled wings, and by night the tawny owl takes over; I know of one who can hoot all night long. If the birds are silent, the ubiquitous wind rarely is, whistling and moaning, rattling tiles on my roof and whiplashing about my walls.

I am attended to by a caretaker during the autumn and winter months. He resides in the service section with his family and the furniture in the main part is dust-sheeted. There is no shelter or respite for me on this summit; gales and rain assail the moors for much of the year and snow falls heavily in the coldest months. When it is deep enough to bury the heather it is rather beautiful. The Butter Road becomes impassable and the moor is a bleak romance of white where dirty sheep toil for blades of grass and are eventually shepherded away to lower slopes. Often the skies are clear at these times and I think

Hudson would admire the 360-degree view of hills and mountains thrown into stark relief by a raiment of pure white. It magnifies the distant hills and all is one great uniform land of snow and ice for a while. During these months the sun traces a lower and shorter path and if Hudson were to sit in his favourite chair in the library, he would find that the sun would be quite blindingly in his eyes, obstructing his favoured view of the moor. He would be better sitting in the south-facing dining room to get the best of the winter sun.

The manager of The Sportsman's Arms and my caretaker are brothers, known as John and James Evans. They bring papers up and discuss the news between them over tea, following the political life of their master and his friends with avid interest.

It is November and the Lords are continuing to frustrate the Liberal Party. They have thrown out the latest Education bill and now the Licensing Bill. The Pensions Bill is the only significant legislation that has made it through in recent times. James can't work out why, but John takes pleasure in telling him that it is because the Pensions Bill was seen to be financial.

'They can't mess about with money issues. That is the job of the Commons only. It would be unconstitutional,' says John wisely.

13

Gwen

March 1954

My brother is not the easiest person to persuade.

'We have to go back and get Alis,' I tell him.

'My torch battery has run out,' says Dewi. 'You can go back in there in the dark if you want, but I'm not. It's too creepy.'

Sometimes I just cannot understand Dewi. He can be so blasé. There I used it. It's a new word and I like learning new words. There are certain words that just sound good and once I know what they mean I store them up and whisper them and say them in my head. Then I'm just waiting for a chance to use them.

'You're so nonchalant, Dewi.'

'What *are* you talking about?'

That's another of my words.

'And I suppose you've forgotten you have another sister,' I say.

'How could I ever forget?'

'Well how do you think she feels?'

'She isn't scared of anything.'

'I bet she's terrified.'

'She's probably out by now. She will have realised that we have played a trick on her and she will be in bed.'

'We have to make this right or we are going to be in big trouble with Mam and Tad when they find out.'

Dewi sighs. He's not so nonchalant now.

'We have my torch and in case that runs out, we can borrow Tad's hurricane lantern,' I say.

'Okay, if you get it. You have quieter feet. And take that necklace off before anyone else sees it.'

I hide the necklace in my pocket and leave him lazing on his bed. What a coward. I'm the one who is most scared of the dark, so that must make me the bravest. But he's right about me being quiet and I'm a good climber too. Maybe I could be a cat burglar. Tad keeps his lantern in the pantry which can only be got to through the kitchen. The trouble is, Tad doesn't go to bed very early like Mam does. Mam will be asleep even before us, as soon as it gets dark, but Tad sits under the gaslight doing his work papers or reading, or sometimes playing his own made-up version of chess against himself with an old set we found in the other-house. Some of the pieces are chipped, but he said they don't make them like that anymore. He thinks they are made of bone. I'm glad it is not ivory as my teacher said elephants have to be killed to get that. Still I suppose an animal died for the bone, but maybe it was an animal that had to be killed anyway for food. Oh, why am I thinking about this now? I hate thinking about things like that but Mam says I have to eat meat. Sometimes I just give it to the dog when no one is looking. Tad knows it's me setting off the mouse traps too. I put my foot in them. Once I nearly broke a toe. I always try to set them off when no one is nearby, otherwise they hear and they know it's me.

I'm nearly at the kitchen door now and my breathing is a bit loud and my heart is thundering in my ears. There is a light shining under the door but I cannot hear anything when I put my ear to the wood. Maybe Tad has gone to bed and accidentally left the light on. What can I say if he is in there? I just want a drink of water. That will do. He might tell me off, but he will probably let me have a drink. And if he's not there, I can get the lantern. Alis is alone in the dark and I've got to help her. I'm so bad to her sometimes and now I feel awfully guilty. I won't be able to sleep unless I sort it out.

I push the door open and the blooming thing creaks so loudly that I stop and leave it at a crack. The crack is enough for me to hear the sound of a knife on a plate.

'Who goes there?' says my Tad's voice.

Damn it.

'It's just me,' I say in my tiniest, most innocent voice. I think I might be Tad's favourite because he gets a lot of cheek off Dewi and he thinks Alis is a bit weird sometimes, but I'm just his princess.

'Come in del, what is it? Nightmares again?'

He is in a good mood.

I push the door open and enter the kitchen. He is sitting at the table buttering a piece of bread. Mam complains sometimes that he eats too much and he has a habit of raiding the pantry at night.

I nod. I may as well pretend it was a bad dream.

'Here, have some bread. It will settle you down and help you sleep. Want some milk too?'

I nod again and he motions for me to join him at the table. This is the best time of the day for Tad.

I heard him say it once; he likes it when everyone is quiet and sleeping. His hurricane lantern is on the table with a fat candle burning in the middle of it. I look at it and wonder if I should tell him about Alis. Maybe I could blame it all on Dewi. No, perhaps not. Dewi would make my life hell. I will try to tell him in a few minutes. First I just want to enjoy a little time in the kitchen, eating bread and drinking milk, with Tad being nice to me.

'What was the dream about?' he asks.

I point to my mouth to show him that I can't speak. Table manners. And it gives me time to think about what to say. In the end I decide to tell him about a real dream I had a few days ago.

'There is a portrait in the other-house. One of a lady who looks a bit scary. I think her name is Selina. I dream that she comes out of the portrait and she shouts at me. She shouts because this is her house and I shouldn't be here. She tells me to get out. She keeps asking, who I am, over and over, and she chases me. There are lots of other people, the ones from the other portraits. They all just stand around drinking wine, staring down at me and laughing loudly. No one wants to help me. They are all telling me to leave. The angry lady is chasing me. I can't run very fast and I think she'll catch me. It's like my feet are stuck in a bog, they're all slow and heavy. That's all I remember.'

'It's just your imagination,' says Tad. 'Nothing to worry about. Anyway, she was a Lady something or other and folk in those days were more polite. They wouldn't have behaved that way.'

He chews his bread thoughtfully.

'Shall I cut us another slice? What about that glass of milk?'

I nod. This is fun.

'I think I know the picture you mean,' he continues. 'I will take it down tomorrow.'

'Will that make her more angry?' I say.

Tad darts a look at me and I realise I just said the sort of thing that Alis would say.

'It's just a picture, *cariad*. It isn't real. I'll take the whole lot down and put them away. Mayhap someone will want them some day.'

'Are they still alive?'

'Who?'

'The people in the paintings.'

'I heard that the children are, but not the parents.'

'The lady I dreamed about is dead?'

'Yes.'

Living people can't be ghosts, but a dead person could come back and haunt their old house. I think this, but I don't say it as Tad will think I'm as mad as my sister.

'See that painting over the fireplace,' says Tad. He points as he chews his bread.

'Yes.'

'We think one of the family painted it. It's signed MK or HK, can't quite make it out. Who knows, these paintings might be worth something.'

I go over for a closer look.

'I never noticed it before.' I say. 'Our home looks like a haunted house, and it's MK I think.'

'It's quite good, don't you think?'

'Yes,' I say. 'I love painting, but we don't get to do it much in school. Teacher doesn't like the mess.'

'It's your birthday soon,' says Tad and winks.

The gaslight is making a funny noise so he turns it off and the kitchen is suddenly a lot darker with just the lantern.

'Saving gas,' he says, as if he needs to explain. 'I don't suppose this place will ever get electricity now.'

I look at the kitchen window, it's just a black pane in the dark with us reflected in it. I see us sitting at the table by the candle, like moths around a light. I lift my glass of milk and the other me does too, so I raise it to her in a toast. Tad sees and laughs, then he does the same.

'Let's see who can drink the quickest,' I say.

'Easy,' he says and before I've even taken a gulp, he throws it back and it's all gone just like that, down his throat, while I'm gulping like a frog. He laughs at me as I start hiccupping, but I think I see something behind our reflection. Passing by the window; a whitish blur. The reflection of Tad and me with the hurricane lantern stops me from seeing clearly. I grab Tad's arm.

'I saw something!'

'Where?'

'Out there,' I point.

Tad looks.

'It's gone now.'

'I only see our reflection in the window,' says Tad. 'What do you think you saw?'

All of a sudden he sounds tired.

'I don't know. It was just like someone walking past.'

That's when I remember Alis.

He gets up and walks heavily to the window; leans forward and with his hand shading his eyes, presses his face close to the glass and looks out.

'Can't see anything,' he concludes. 'Maybe it was a fox.'

Why do foxes get blamed for everything? But I keep quiet. I have remembered Alis and now I feel scared. If I tell Tad he might be angry especially as he is getting tired now and the fun is over, but at least he could be relied on to sort it out. I can't go back into the other-house, not after seeing that. I'm much too scared now.

'Come on, I'll walk you back up to bed.'

'Okay.'

The moment passes, my tongue sticks—all dry—to the roof of my mouth. Poor Alis. I tell myself that she is probably back in her bed like Dewi said before. As Tad tucks me in and says the bedbug rhyme, I really believe that. But when he has gone and turned the light out, I know it's rubbish because after being left like that Alis would not have gone to bed quietly. She would have been angry.

14

I wake feeling a bit odd. It is hard to say how long I slept. I only remember thinking I would never be able to sleep, but I must have because here I am now, lying in my bed trying to work out what time it is from the clock on the wall. Is it six o'clock or half past twelve? As my mind starts to wake up, I see that it's just getting light. Then I remember the business with Alis and my heart sinks. The episode in the kitchen with Tad last night eating bread by candlelight returns too. A good memory, but I brush it aside for later. I can't feel happy until I know that Alis is okay. Until then there is only this nasty, creepy feeling of peril. Peril. That's another of the words I like. But I don't like it so much now that I can use it. I have to wake Dewi.

Dewi is very hard to wake. He is sleeping with his head and arms thrown back and his mouth wide open. Letting out little snores. I open his curtains to let in the light. It's quite bright with the snow even though it's foggy out there and the sun is hidden. I shake him vigorously and he groans, then he starts flailing his arms at me and fighting back as if he's in a dream and I am an attacker. This makes me laugh for a moment, but only for a moment because I keep thinking of Alis.

'Wake up, Dewi, damn you!' I say in my loudest whisper.

Just as I'm thinking of pouring water over him like they do in one of our comic books, his eyes open and he looks at me with a sort of angry confusion.

'What in hell,' he says.

'Hold your tongue,' I whisper and I place my hand over his mouth. This makes him even angrier. He pulls my hand off and gives me his maddest look. I want to laugh.

'We left Alis all night,' I remind him. 'We have to go and find her now before Mam and Tad get up!'

Thank goodness he listens for once. He must have fallen asleep while he was waiting for me last night, but he is ready to act now. Lucky for us it is Saturday and our parents will probably have a lie-in.

'Yes, if we get to her first we might be able to do a deal with her,' he whispers as he gets up, stumbles and then pulls his dressing gown on.

I nod. It might be possible but I think Alis would demand a high price from us. If she's still with us. But I brush that thought away.

'Let's check her bedroom first,' says Dewi. 'I looked last night after you'd gone, but she wasn't in there. What happened to you anyway?'

I explain in whispers as we walk down the narrow corridor to the end bedroom. Mam said it used to be a housemaid's room, but now it's Alis's. She's not there though. Silly us for even hoping it would be that simple. I feel queasy but we press on. We don't need to talk. We have to go into the other-house, but at least it's light now.

We follow the route from yesterday. When we reach the dining room where the portraits are, I pause to look at them all. It's strange how they sometimes look different. Selina doesn't look angry today, but reproachful. Reproachful, that's another good word I've learned. Lloyd George normally has a hint of a smile, but not today. Now he looks annoyed. Hudson looks the same as usual, a proud man with a moustache that almost reaches across his whole face and narrowed eyes, looking at us suspiciously.

In the middle of the two younger men—Gerald and Mark Kearley—is a young woman. Beryl. Her dark hair and eyes are shining. She's the only one who isn't angry with us. I like her the best.

'Do you think she's beautiful?' I ask.

'Don't you want to find Alis?' says Dewi. 'We haven't got all day.'

'Yes, you're right.'

I try not to look at Selina Kearley. I imagine she ruled the house and no one dared to be cheeky to her. 1911 is the date on the paintings; more than forty years ago.

We climb the stairs and I look sadly at the lumps of wallpaper that Dewi and Alis ripped off yesterday. The paintings pass out of my mind and all I can think about now is whether we'll find our sister.

I take the lead because I know which room it is. The one Alis showed me, the one with a chest in it. I push the door and it swings open silently. The first thing I see is the snowy moors outside the window. Beneath the window is the chest. It looks tatty in the morning light. Dewi pushes past me, pointing at the gold catch that we both notice only now.

I put my hand to my mouth without thinking. I don't know what to feel. Dread, horror or shock, but even as Dewi undoes the catch and lifts the lid, I know already that Alis isn't in the chest, so it's unnecessary and a bit silly when Dewi exclaims about her not being there.

'It smells bad in there,' he says.

I stay by the door, frozen.

'What now?' he asks me. The colour has drained from his face and he is looking to me to lead.

'I don't know.'

I look around the room. I walk to the curtains and lift them, shaking them so that clouds of dust are set off. It feels ridiculous to even think that she would be hiding in the curtains but I don't know where else to look, the room is empty except for the chest. I even open the chest and look in there again, as if I think it might have a false bottom like those magician's ones do. Alis might have found her way into a cavity or secret passageway below. Of course I'm fantasising, the chest is quite shallow and small and there is nothing unusual about it; although I notice a damp patch on its base and a whiff of something unpleasant as I close it.

'We have to search all of the other-house,' I decide. 'And if we don't find her, then we go back and search our part.'

'And then what?' Dewi asks.

There are twelve other bedrooms, two dressing rooms, three bathrooms and several en-suites to search in this part of the house. We look but she isn't anywhere. As we search I keep thinking I hear noises, not in the room we're in, but in the next one. I tell Dewi to be quiet and we both stand still, but as soon as we listen, the house is silent, its stillness a counterpart to the snowy scene outside.

'You're hearing things,' says Dewi.

Downstairs there is the inner staircase hall and the outer hall by the front door. I test the heavy oak doors to see if they have been opened recently.

'Why are you doing that?' Dewi asks.

'Alis was good at opening doors,' I say.

But these are locked fast.

We look at the fireplace and then at each other. I suppose it was nice in the olden days to have a fireplace in the front hall to welcome visitors and perhaps it kept the servants warm too as they waited at the doors. I don't know when the fire was last used but it wasn't cleaned and there's a film of ash around it on the parquet floor. And footprints in the ash.

We look at each other again but neither of us wants to say anything. Of course we know the footprints are Alis's.

'She's always wandering about,' says Dewi, his voice has changed and sounds more blasé. 'And she sleepwalks.'

I nod, but I look back all the same at the little footprints by the fire. I feel some heaviness, I suppose it's guilt.

We head back through the inner hall into the dining room. It's a large room with a big fireplace. This one is clean. I move the curtains again. They are faded and damp and the window is broken. I wonder why I think our sister is still playing hide and seek with us?

In the library, a chicken clucks suspiciously from beneath the small stack of furniture covered by a cloth. I see a few chairs with curved legs, a small oval table and a pretty glass trolley. The tin box is on the trolley where Alis left it.

'I want the brooch too,' I say, opening the box.

'Do you want to be a witch or something?' says Dewi. 'Isn't that necklace creepy enough for you?'

'I am a witch,' I say. 'I am wearing the necklace already.'

'I can't see it.'

'It's under my clothes. It has more power if it's warm.'

'You're making it up,' says Dewi, but he looks a bit unsettled by the way I'm glaring at him with my witch eyes.

'Come on,' he says, as he steps away from me. 'We need to find Alis.'

I fix the brooch to my jumper and decide it will be a talisman to protect me. We continue our search. No Alis, of course, but looking is something to do. It's delaying the moment when we have to give up and tell our parents.

On we go, looking in the empty cabinet in the gun room and arguing about whether Alis would have climbed out of one of the broken windows.

'Even she wasn't crazy enough to do that,' says Dewi.

In the cloakroom, Dewi decides to take a wee in the toilet.

The drawing room at the front of the house is cold and the pale mist at the windows is all I can see. We don't come in this room much, although it is right next to our part of the house, you can't reach it from the connecting corridor, only from the hallway near the front door. It gets the morning sun on the days when it's clear. There is a fireplace and thick curtains, and the windows aren't broken here at least. It is empty except for a dusty armchair by the fire and a painting on the wall. The painting is quite small and now I look more closely, I see MK in the corner. It's of a lady in a long purplish dress and white shawl. She stands proudly on the moor, surrounded by brown heather. As I look at her, I realise that it's Beryl, and in the background there is a more blurry figure, that looks like a man. He's too far away to be clear, it's as if he is part of the moor itself. I have seen this painting before, but never really looked closely as it's a bit high on the wall.

When I look at Dewi, he is frowning at me.

'Do you think it's a ghost?' he asks.

'What?'

'That figure in the painting.'

'Maybe. It looks like she doesn't know it's there.'

'And it's all smoky, it doesn't look real.'

We continue our search. Other smaller rooms and cupboards reveal nothing either.

'It's as if Alis was never here,' I say, but I'm really talking about the feeling of emptiness I get from the other-house.

'We have to search our part now.'

'Yes,' I agree.

'What about the cellar?'

I hadn't thought about the cellar. It's not all that pleasant. Stone steps lead down from our part of the house into a dark brick passageway, which takes you into a large underground room with wooden shelves, low ceilings and cobwebs where large spiders lurk, scuttling out and prodding their legs on their webs at the slightest vibration. I shudder at the thought of the cellar with its cold and heavy air, odours of moulds, fungi, mouse and moss. There's lots of old stuff down there. Tad says it's mostly tins and packets of old food left over from World War II when the house was used for some sort of training. He thinks it used to be a wine and beer cellar for the family before that, but that is all long gone.

'We will tell Mam and Tad before we go into the cellar,' I decide.

Dewi smirks at me. He knows too well that I am afraid of spiders.

We search our part of the house, slowly. We are dawdling as if we have the power to slow time down. Maybe if we go slowly enough, time will start to go backwards and we could change everything. We could find Alis and pull her out of the chest and say sorry. Better still, we would never even play the trick on her. It was a just a bad choice that we made. Do bad choices end up making a bad person? My teacher at school talked about the consequences of our actions in assembly. I didn't understand it then. Sometimes you have to do things yourself in order to understand.

As I search under my bed, I hear the door open behind me. It's Mam.

'What are you doing?' she asks.

15

Hudson

2nd August 1913

I don't just come here to shoot, though I confess that I chose this area partly for the habitat that is good for sporting. My dear, now deceased friend and fellow MP, Tom Ellis said that for him, the birds could all live their lives out in peace without a shot ever being fired. I don't tend towards that kind of sentimentality myself though I respected him for it and perhaps in penance for lives taken here, I have made my beautiful garden at Wittington a haven for songbirds where no shooting or trapping of any bird is permitted. I tolerate them taking fruits and seeds and like to think of myself as their friend. I am not without compassion for other living things and confess that after my one big-game hunting trip, I had no taste for another and though I eat the flesh of other beings, I speak for standards and systems that provide for their welfare. Once, on a visit to Chicago, in the United States—a trip I enjoyed in an amazing country, but one that was not without its ugliness—I admit to being shocked at seeing a collapsed cow left on an unloading platform at an animal market. At the time I asked the men there what had happened. I was answered with words to the effect that many hogs and cattle die in transportation. Several hours later, I passed the same spot to see the animal still there, still suffering what appeared to be a slow death.

'What is going to be done about this?' I asked the only person I could find nearby.

When he didn't answer me I asked him if this was normal. He just shrugged and said that was just the way things were done. If I had had my gun I might have furnished the creature with a quicker end, but I did not and I was left thinking that the people of Chicago need to do better than allow such unnecessary suffering. It got me thinking about how no system is perfect. I have learned that through my own industry in creating more efficient food retail systems and I have been forced to learn it again in government. Britain also has many systems that are traditional, time-honoured, habitual and quite frankly, totally ineffective, inept and bungling. We are particularly fond of our conventional and customary ways of doing things, no matter how outmoded and covered in thick dust and perverse stubbornness they might be. In reality change is the only constant thing and one must embrace it.

My children are sitting with me. The maid has cleared breakfast away and it is one of those rare times when we are together in companionable silence. We are having better than average weather and have made it out onto the south-facing terrace at Gwylfa. There is barely a breeze to ruffle my papers. Gerald has a novel and Beryl is reading the local press. Mark faces the opposite way and sits a little away from us at his easel, painting. He has quite a talent. I get up and take a look every now and again to see how his composition is progressing. It's a vibrant display of manifold colour in oil. He has the sky and heather in the exact hue as they are, but the house I feel looks a little dark and sombre, though he has depicted the shape and imposing demeanour well.

I return to my seat and sit back to enjoy the unencumbered open space. We have a party planned and one of the guests is Dei. I'm glad he's able to come as I don't see him much now that I'm at the Port of London, but I do still keep up with the politics of the Liberal Party as well as I can.

Lloyd George's Budget League conspired to link the budget to social reforms, to prevent the Lords from using their power of veto. It was the 1909 People's Budget that finally broke the Upper House; their attempt to stop it meant interfering in matters beyond their remit. They who had relished their place as superior folk and the proper owners and rulers of the land, nation and empire, now felt the ground shaking beneath them. Their anger after Lloyd George's infamous Limehouse speech, led to an intervention from the King asking Asquith if Lloyd George could be restrained. When the Lords threw the budget out, the government was dissolved and a general election called.

Despite our efforts to improve democracy, the general election in 1910 saw us losing seats and having to form a minority government with the backing of the Irish Nationalists and the Labour Party; but against all odds, our defeat of the House of Lords was completed in 1911 with the Parliament Act, whereupon the Lords retained their power of veto but parliament was given the final say as it always should have done. How we celebrated that one and how our enemies seethed. Winston Churchill, in particular was disliked for having gone against his upper class roots.

For my part, the last few years have been mixed with blessings and trials, I was ill for several months in 1909 with phlebitis and missed some of the excitements of that year, but recovered well. My work at the Port of London has proven to be challenging but worthy, and I have felt enthused by it and rather regarded it as a big adventure.

1913 has been a more difficult year for the government with growing unrest over the implacable Irish problem and violent protests from the suffragettes. It is a relief then to have this break and a party to look forward to.

*

The footman has been busy at the door, welcoming visitors for our luncheon party since last evening, but they are almost all here now. Dei has brought his young daughter Megan and his secretary. They are not staying for the shooting tomorrow, though a few of the other guests are.

It is one of those days when the moor is at its best and I love my guests to see it, so we are eating outside on the south-facing terrace. Selina is supervising the set, while I'm standing at the end of the terrace looking out at the heather. I can see the insects buzzing about the millions of tiny purple flowers. I love my garden in Wittington and have put much of myself into it, but a garden wouldn't be quite right here in this rather primeval place. I prefer to enjoy the pristine air and the wild heath as it is. It has a certain magic, I think. Small birds fly about the heather, hunting the insects. If I had my field-glasses I could see what they are, but I suspect they are meadow pipits. The agile swallows are among my favourites of course, I envy how they skim the heather in long sweeping circles, changing direction with a slight turn of their narrow shoulders, their glossy wings like blades.

I turn to find the footman on the terrace.

'Gilbert Augustus Tonge is here.'

'Ah good, I was worried he would be late, he said he might be.' I follow him.

Gilbert Tonge is my business partner and our success I feel, is partly down to our long and happy relations. We have always been in perfect accord. We own International Stores together and I am happy to see him in a social setting for a change. We do this too infrequently since I relinquished my involvement in the business for a political career. Public life has been a breath of air for me, while it is anathema to Gilbert, who still runs the business. I have things I want to discuss with him but wonder if luncheon with other guests will provide an opportunity. Perhaps we can get away together for a little while.

We shake hands and grip each other's shoulder. He's a smart-looking man with owlish eyes and a long nose. He is clean-shaven and his mouth looks a little grim, until he smiles.

'Lovely to have you with us,' I say. 'Come out onto the terrace with me.'

I hope that my chance to talk with him might come about now, but as we pass through the dining room, we are spotted by my great friend Tim Healey and his wife Erina.

'Say Hudson. We were just admiring your beautiful carvings on this fireplace,' says Erina. 'What wood is it?'

'Oak,' I say. 'Have you met Gilbert Tonge?'

They have, once before, briefly in London.

Tim and Erina follow us out so I am unable to raise the subject I wanted with Gilbert.

'Is the house now finished at last?' says Erina as we walk around it.

I note the hint of what might be sarcasm, but choose to ignore it.

'I believe it is,' I answer and look towards Gwylfa with pride. 'It is no longer our creaky old Plas Pren that leaked like a sieve. I wondered at times whether those Norwegians put it together properly, but now I have no doubt that it will last and it has lost that uncouth look that it had. There is nothing left to do.'

'Who gave it that name and what does it mean?' asks Erina. I notice that she is always full of questions, usually asked with her cigarette holder poised and her head tilted to one side.

'I don't remember,' I say, though I think it might have been Dei. 'And Plas Pren means wooden palace.'

Erina splutters a bit as she laughs.

'The plaque reads 1913,' says Tim, 'that means there can be no more additions.'

'What's the Latin on it?' Erina asks.

'Strength is the way,' I reply.

'The way to what?'

'—to build your house high,' says Tim.

It doesn't matter if they chafe me. I am happy with the house. Its countenance is more favourable. It looks dignified. Before, it had some quality that I found upsetting, not exactly evil, but muddled and discordant and there was that recurring dream, which appears to have stopped now.

'Why did you paint it white though?' asks Erina.

'To make it stand out. And to preserve it. It's lighthouse paint, you know. Houses on hills have to be maintained. There is no shelter here.'

'We think it's a great improvement,' says Selina, from the table nearby.

'It's the work of my architect, Jacobean in style,' I say. 'The large mullioned windows make best use of the light.'

'The views are incredible,' says Tim, 'it's almost clear enough to see Ireland.'

He looks out towards the west and I wonder if he's a little homesick.

'Indeed, I had to hire a psychic, three different long-range meteorologists and an astrologer to find the perfect day for this party,' I say, and they laugh.

The food is ready so we retire to the terrace where a long table has been set up with white cloths and Selina's favourite luncheon service. The china one edged in a gold and dark red leaf pattern with a sugar bowl that's almost as big as the teapot. Selina loves the gorgeous looped handle on top.

Our other guests are seating themselves, along with my three children. I look with interest at Dei's secretary and realise it's the same young woman that used to be governess to his daughter Megan. She was a friend of Mair's too. She's quite a handsome creature, although not as striking as Beryl who sits next to her. I notice my wife is looking at her too and then she looks at me with raised eyebrows. Little Megan is happy at least, she appears to be comfortable sitting with her father and this Frances.

'How goes the Port of London?' asks Gilbert as we all take seats.

'It keeps me busy,' I say.

'And out of the cabinet,' says Tim and when I look at him sharply, he adds: 'more's the pity.'

'That ship sailed from the docks long ago,' I say and marvel at my own witticism.

'You could still come back in,' says Dei.

'I have my work cut out where I am,' I say. 'I told Asquith it would be a full-time job and it has not disappointed in that respect. He wanted to put me in the cabinet, it's true, and maybe he was a little sad that he hadn't done so years before when there was a chance.'

'Well, I told you at the time you need to canvass your friends. Put the pressure on. It was clear he felt guilty for leaving you out. I wanted you in, you know that,' says Dei, as the servants bring the bouillon to the table.

'There's no point in going over it now,' I say, feeling a tendril of anger uncurling in me.

Dei continues to smile mischievously at me.

'Have you got good people working for you there?' asks Tim and I turn gratefully towards him.

'Yes, for the most part. I wanted good business-minded people rather than the usual type of civil servant. In my years in business and government, I've come to know that I can only rely on twenty-five per cent of my employees to take their duties seriously in any business. The rest have but a moderate interest and engagement, often coupled with inferior knowledge of the business as a result.'

'I agree, come to think of it,' says Gilbert. 'Perhaps not exactly with those figures, but close.'

'Have you found a way to increase engagement above that twenty–five per cent?' asks Erina.

'Not really, but then I'm not sure I'd want one-hundred percent passionately involved because it would be sure to lead to much conflict, such is human nature. Conflict would in turn lead to a lowering of enthusiasm and dissipation of energies. However, I do find a problem with the other seventy-five per cent when it comes to casting a vote. All votes count equally, but often those who have not given their all, are somewhat timid and short-sighted to a fault and become a deadweight to progressive policy. This stagnant and reactionary response holds us back. Indeed it's been my main battle to keep the authority as forward-thinking, progressive and long-sighted as I can. This has been necessary for our main aim.'

'And what is that?' asks Erina.

'To bring the Port of London up to modern standards and to make provision for expansion, there is enough work there to keep us busy for many years.'

I pause as a servant offers me the platter of chicken timbales. The smell is quite delicious and I motion for two.

'London must modernise but she is still the centre of the world,' says Erina, taking salmon sandwiches from the platter. 'But I have often wondered where is the centre of London? It's quite haphazard don't you think?'

'It has developed organically and without design,' says Dei. 'Now look at Paris, there is a city of beauty but then it was mostly rebuilt to achieve those lines.'

'It was a cesspit before,' says Tim.

'I often think it's almost as if we accidentally acquired this great empire and became the centre of world commerce without really planning it,' I say as I bite into a timbale. It's necessary to wipe my chin after with a napkin.

'That cook of yours is a genius,' says Gilbert, noticing my gaffe.

'London is without a plan,' says Erina. 'She just keeps sprawling further out and swallowing up villages and towns as she goes. But where is the centre?' she repeats her question.

'The centre is the banking sector, the heart of business and commerce,' I say. 'That's where most of the activity of London is and where a lot of the work is concentrated.'

'I disagree,' says Gilbert and I look up at the man in surprise. He's disagreeing with me more than he usually does. In fact I'm not sure that he ever disagrees with me.

'It's in the west,' he says, 'the seat of government and the monarchy, where Nelson's column rises up. That's the heart of it. You should have said that, being a man of government yourself.'

'Perhaps it is more realistically a city of many hearts and many centres,' says Dei, 'for I do not feel when I walk into number 11 that I am in the very centre of the great metropolis. For me there is more than one centre depending on which London you want to find.'

'What do you mean exactly?' I ask.

'I mean that perhaps there is a London city of finance, but there is also a city of culture and art, and as Gilbert said the city of government, heart of an empire. And what of the thousands of anonymous souls who live there and work there, often in poor conditions, what London do they see? It is different again for them. Maybe the opportunities of the city are an insurmountable brick wall to them, who merely survive in dark hovels and dread the call of the poor house. I cannot but wonder at what would be the centre for them.'

'Probably the seat of government as it is for us,' argues Tim. 'Or the banking sector. Just because it's unattainable doesn't stop them seeing it as the heart of things.'

'What does our business man say? Is London in decline or will she be the centre of the world for years to come?' Gilbert asks me.

I shift in my seat and answer as well as I can: 'Who can guess? You know as well as I, Gilbert that our country is still a great exporter, but an exporter in decline and a brisk trade in financial products cannot fully replace production and trade of physical goods, but I see a gradual decline rather than a rapid one.'

'And what of our empire?' says Erina.

'What is this? One hundred questions?'

'It will be the last if you can answer it,' she continues, poised with her fork and a bit of speared salmon in the place of the cigarette holder.

'The same. A slow crumbling from within I expect,' I say, feeling myself sit up straighter, 'rather like what happened to the Romans. The same for the French empire, only I think the collapse will be quicker for them since less of their countrymen have taken to living abroad in the colonies, a fact which must surely make their empire weaker than ours.'

'The French have it too good in France, that's why they stay,' says Tim.

As they continue, I find my attention lapses, as it often does when there are too many people to attend to. I watch the servants bringing out roast cod with asparagus and parsley sauce, herb potatoes and green bean salad. The operation is smooth and it does not disturb the conversation. The fish is soft and succulent, falling apart in the sauce. Sometimes I think that it would be better to eat in silence to appreciate fully the food. It so appeals to the senses of sight, smell and taste, even to touch as I cut into a soft, floury potato which melts into the sauce. Tim is talking, I don't pay his words any heed, but look at him instead; his proud dark Gaelic head is turning to grey. He nods at someone's input but can barely restrain himself politely before he follows up with a quick comeback. He is a better man to have as friend than enemy. We are not at all alike, he and I, though we can talk all night and feel comfortable in each other's silences too. I am quite out of the conversation and suddenly a little tired, but enjoying the flutter of my guests talking around me, the sound of cutlery clinking on the china and the open moorland setting. I sometimes feel that talking limits us, we miss so much when we only talk incessantly. My wife knows immediately when I'm out for she takes a more active role. I see her now, nodding and putting in some comment. She's a formidable looking woman, yet to those who know her, the sweetest dear.

'Nietzsche has written that Europe wants to become one state,' she is saying, 'I think that is good for our prospects. We are all of us well-travelled and must consider ourselves European and cosmopolitan, even the nationalists within us.'

'Part of nationalism is to want the best for our countries and appreciating what others can offer is part of that,' says Dei.

'I don't believe we can come to war with Europe now that we are quite entangled with our neighbours. It would be uneconomic and deeply unprofitable for all concerned,' Gilbert says. I am glad to see him here taking part, he doesn't generally like parties too much and has a slightly nervous disposition in unfamiliar company, but he seems to be doing very well today.

'Tell that to the hot-blooded Prussians,' says Tim. 'I don't believe they care for the consequences.'

'But haven't Anglo-German relations thawed somewhat since Dei's last visit?' I say. 'Did we not witness a wedding this year with dear old King George swapping clothes with the Kaiser?'

'Don't forget Tsar Nicholas II, he was there too, cousins all three of them with George and the Tsar so alike they could be twins,' says Selina.

'It was more of a puppet show don't you think? A ceremony,' says Erina, I notice her hand is poised theatrically, with nothing in it.

'But is blood thicker than water?' asks Dei. 'I'd say it looked good, except I have some knowledge of the Kaiser and he's not quite as dependable and dull as our old George. A proud and haughty creature that one.'

I wonder if part of the reason for his dislike is the fact that the Kaiser refused to meet with him.

'But he's the Kaiser of 25 years peace isn't he?' says a soft voice from next to Dei. 'Wasn't he nominated for the Nobel Peace Prize?'

It's the first time Frances, Dei's new secretary has spoken and we all look at her for a moment as we consider both her and her contribution.

'Maybe,' says Dei, perhaps to save her as she looks a little embarrassed at the sudden attention. 'But he doesn't fully identify with peace. He has said that war with France is inevitable and he refused to treat with me on the subject of naval proliferation.'

Ah yes, that again.

'Aye and his son openly bays like a hound for a war that will give a young and exuberant nation like Germany its chance against old has-beens like France and Britain,' says Tim.

'Not to mention von Bernhardi's book. He not only predicted war but went on to call for war imminently if Germany is to have any chance of greatness,' says Dei.

'Who is he?'

'A general, now retired.'

'Good that he's retired then.'

'Any war that comes will be quick.'

'And bloody as all wars are.'

'I don't believe it will come to that, and we have worker solidarity across Europe to thank—'

We all stop talking at the sound of a noisy motor, before we realise that it's coming from the sky.

'An aeroplane!' says Beryl and she is the first to jump up and peruse the sky in all directions. We all join her and follow the direction of her pointing finger. 'There!'

It's not much different than the first aeroplane that we ever saw, two years ago over Wittington, but perhaps the original box kite look has grown a bit sleeker and it doesn't look as if it's about to fall from the sky. I laugh as I note how all our arms are waving frantically—it's the same every time— but I join in anyway, even as I want to question it.

'He waved back,' shouts Beryl, above the clatter. I didn't see that myself, but resist the temptation to argue with her in front of our guests; perhaps her youthful vision is better than mine.

The machine retreats and I am glad to see the back of the tedious thing. The sky returns to its former trackless quiet and a mournful buzzard soars on thermals over the moor as if the aeroplane never came.

We are onto our puddings now: angel parfait, finger cakes and bonbons.

'If there was to be a war, would they fight it using planes?' asks Mark.

'I hope not,' I say. 'I'm not sure those things are quite developed enough to fly long distances.'

'Someone flew across the Mediterranean in one this summer,' says Gerald.

'Yes,' I say. 'Some*one*. Not some-many.'

'Yes and didn't that Samuel Cody die when he crashed his plane recently?' says Tim.

'He did,' Dei agrees. 'Just a few weeks ago and he was an experienced flier, the first to fly a plane over Britain.'

'You won't get me up there, I'm afraid,' says Erina.

'Anyway, we're far too friendly with everyone these days,' says Selina. 'We're on good terms with the French, the Americans and now the Germans. Why, the Prince of Wales is on a motoring trip up the Rhine as we speak.'

'And I'm planning a trip to the Bavarian Alps,' says Mark. 'A friend and I hope to go next year for the summer.'

'Globalisation,' I say. 'The world is getting smaller and more prosperous. It's an easier journey abroad now than ever we could have dreamed of a few decades back and there's talk of building a tunnel through to France so we'll be able to drive a motor or take a train to Europe before long.'

'Better than braving the English Channel in winter,' says Gilbert.

'Personally I think we've made an error in getting too close diplomatically with France,' says Tim.

'Why?' I ask.

'They'll think they've got us with a blank cheque when it comes to settling scores with Germany.'

'We'd be better staying out of any conflict in Europe,' says Erina.

'Churchill wouldn't agree, he's busy planning it all. A master strategist that one,' says Tim. 'Although, you did well getting him into the admiralty, Dei, they needed a shake up.'

'He's ever one for a fight,' I say. 'While Dei was negotiating with the strikers, Churchill was ranting about bringing the military in to crush them.'

'I don't think the Germans would let us stay out of a war if it came to it,' says Tim. 'They've got a score to settle with us.'

I find myself looking at Dei, he is nodding but too engaged with his pudding to speak. In fact, I am finding him a little less lively than usual, although he is contributing, he isn't dominating. I look at the two women at his side and wonder if he is behaving because of them.

'—but let's be more positive,' Erina is saying. 'Germany's social reforms are to be admired at least—'

'Even if the rest of their politics is to be condemned,' says Tim.

'And,' Erina continues, with a glaring look in the direction of the dissenting voice of her husband, 'we have much to learn from them in spite of our government's progress with pensions and National Insurance.'

Dei doesn't rise to the bait, or perhaps he doesn't get the chance because it's his daughter Megan who speaks then, and I realise it's the first time she's spoken.

'We've talked a lot about war but what do we think about the suffragettes?' she asks. For an eleven-year-old, she's a bright spark and I can see something of his energy and his love of the limelight living on in her. She may not be the beauty that Mair was, but she possesses the same intense blue eyes as her dashing father, and has been the pet of Downing Street since she moved there at the age of five.

Selina groans. 'Don't make us say. If there's one issue that is guaranteed to split households and turn friend against friend it's that one.'

'Maybe,' says Frances, and again we all look as she speaks, 'but despite its many supposed supporters, don't you think it's rather become a political orphan?'

'What do you mean?' Selina asks.

'Well, a private bill is not enough to get it through parliament, it needs a government to take it on, but so far no government has.'

She rather earnestly looks about the table as if in search of a candidate.

'Don't look at me,' I say humorously, 'your employer is the Chancellor after all.'

'And Lloyd George is a supporter of women's right to the vote,' she says, looking sideways at him with a delicate, slightly unsure smile. I guess in that moment that women's suffrage means something to this young lady. And I guess something else in the way he twinkles back at her, his moustache isn't big enough to hide the smile he bestows in return.

'His support didn't stop the suffragettes from blowing up his new house,' I say.

There is a short silence as everyone looks at me and then at Dei.

Dei's smile has evaporated. 'No, indeed,' he says. 'It was unfortunate that they chose to blow my house up. It seems they think I'm not doing enough, but it's a little difficult when the Prime Minister is completely opposed to the women's vote and the party is divided. The suffragettes don't seem to appreciate that.'

'Aye,' says Tim. 'And many influential women have spoken against women voting which has made it difficult for any government.'

'Some of the suffragists, including a few who are prominent, are undecided in the support of their own cause and have shown themselves to be opponents of the liberal government first and foremost, and take every opportunity to disrupt my public appearances for that reason only.'

'Really?' says Erina, she sounds a little doubtful.

'Oh yes,' says Dei, his jaw is set and he is ready for a fight if needed. 'I have had occasion to observe certain characters happily supporting Conservative members who are opposed to the women's vote. What other conclusion can I draw here?'

'He has been hounded unfairly,' says Tim. 'Even Pankhurst seems to like Asquith better than Dei, but Asquith is completely opposed to the vote. It's an oddity don't you think?'

'People are quick to call any Welshman a slippery serpent. Perhaps it is our flag,' Dei laughs.

'I think it is the finest flag in the kingdom,' says Megan proudly.

'Perhaps they think me a liar,' says Dei.

'The dragon has two tongues,' says Tim.

'I think it's because you do support it and they think you should resign from a government that doesn't,' says Erina.

'That's a narrow-minded view of things. I believe I can do more good by staying and in all seriousness, I think it important that women play a greater role, they have more idea of the country's social needs,' Dei says. 'Housing and education reform are needed, not to mention slum clearance. I believe women would be great advocates for these.'

'I'm still waiting for an answer from the rest of you,' says little Megan smartly.

We are distracted from giving her what she wants by the appearance of my old friend Ralph leaning heavily on his stick. He's not been well and had a tray taken to his room but I guess that he cannot resist the entertainment. Luckily, a footman is on hand to bring him a chair. He waves him away as he tries to fuss and sits down heavily.

'What's the pudding?' he asks.

'Didn't you have any?' asks Selina.

'I did, but I fancy seconds. Oh, a bonbon will do. And some coffee.'

Megan regards the elderly guest and asks him what he thinks about women's suffrage. I can't help smiling at this little sprite.

'I don't agree,' says Ralph and pops a bonbon in his mouth.

'For my part I've always supported women's right to vote,' I say. 'But I can't condone the use of this cause for other political ends nor can I support the activities of some of the extremists in the movement. 1913 has certainly been a busy year for them.'

'Indeed,' says Dei. 'Despite Asquith's opposition, most of the cabinet was in support of women's suffrage, but that has decreased this year with the shocking violence. I myself am still a supporter, but I feel the cause is lost for the time being. No government can be seen to bow to violence.'

'Like that disgraceful nonsense at the Derby,' says Ralph suddenly. He's raised his head so abruptly that he's lost his eyeglass in the process. 'That was an educated woman and not only did she kill herself but put the lives of others in danger. If that is how an educated woman behaves, then perhaps we'd be right in not letting any woman have the vote.'

'Emily Wilding Davison was her name,' says Frances.

'She was one of the two who blew up Dei's house,' I say.

'What is the world coming to with women committing violent acts? What next, will the children rise up?' Ralph exclaims as he takes a bowl of angel parfait and digs his spoon in.

A small silence settles over the table as we all adjust to the presence of Ralph, but I see that his words have garnered the interest of my daughter. I wonder if it is time to withdraw inside for crème de menthe and that talk with Gilbert.

'And men have never committed violent acts to get what they want?' asks Beryl. 'Do men not fight for their rights and freedom?'

'I didn't say that, of course there will always be violent extreme acts, but this is not to be expected from educated women,' says Ralph, reddening a little at the challenge.

Selina stands and we start to move inside to the drawing room. I look back as we go in, it's still a wonderful day and it is comparatively darker indoors.

'—are you saying that an educated woman is not capable of passionate feeling for a cause?' Beryl continues, she's hung back so she can walk in with the men.

'An educated woman should be able to control her passions just as educated men do,' Ralph answers emphatically.

I turn to Gilbert who has fallen in beside me.

'I'd like to talk if we can,' I say.

He nods and looks askance at me.

'Nothing bad,' I say. 'Don't worry.'

'—really. And how many educated men have led their countries to war? Too many to count I fear.'

'—we are in no war now, let it be said that we have learned from the past,' Ralph sounds quite irate.

By the time we reach the drawing room, Beryl's arms are folded and she is glaring at Ralph, but before she can say more, Frances speaks:

'And has not the government made war against the suffragettes with this Cat and Mouse Act?'

'What now? Speak clearly, I don't understand,' snaps Ralph. He has replaced his eyeglass, but I notice the three young ladies laughing as it falls down again and I smile at the way his heavy moustache hides his mouth but moves up and down as he speaks.

'The prison service releases suffragettes who are ill from hunger striking, but then has them re-arrested as soon as they are better.'

'Ah yes,' I say, turning to the little group. 'That is to avoid them dying and to avoid the situation of the government having caused their death. It is really for the good of all, if the suffragettes could but see it.'

'They're avoiding giving them a martyr,' says Frances, so I turn back to Gilbert and try to have my talk with him.

'It's about the future of the business,' I say to him and we move a little away from the argument towards the window. 'I think we need to discuss who might succeed us.'

But I can't quite stop listening to the little group with Ralph. Perhaps someone should help him out, he's only just gotten over illness. Frances is almost as spirited as Beryl and probably nearly the same age.

'Tell the fools to stop their hunger striking then. It's not lady-like,' Ralph's moustache moves and he throws his crème de menthe down in one go.

I turn back to Gilbert. 'I've been sounding out the boys for some time, but in truth I see no interest there. If anything, Beryl would be the one. But no, that cannot be either. I wonder if you have any successor in mind?'

'—the hunger strike is an act of protest which has nothing to do with being lady-like or indeed man-like. They are protesters,' Frances is telling Ralph. 'And they do it so that they will be seen as political prisoners rather than common criminals.'

'Damn fools don't deserve the vote for that.'

'It would be nice for the government, to disallow protesters from having a vote, I'm sure,' says Beryl. 'It won't be good for moral progress though.'

I realise that I haven't listened to what Gilbert is saying and although I am facing him and nodding at him as if listening, my hearing is tuned into what is going on behind me. If I were a horse, my ears would be turned backwards.

'Stop putting words in my mouth, damn it! I meant *violent* protesters,' says Ralph angrily.

I turn away from Gilbert, realising vaguely that I am being rude. 'There is probably no point in arguing with our young womenfolk on this point,' I say. 'The young always want truth and justice to prevail and it is just that women should be allowed to vote.'

Ralph bangs his stick down on the wooden floor and says, 'Humph.'

'But what will you do about it?' asks Megan, turning her bright young eyes onto me.

'Well I'm not in the government anymore, I'm the chairman of the Port of London. You should petition your father.'

'I will support it wherever I go,' says Tim. 'I am already a supporter of the Irish suffragettes.'

'How many do *not* support it?' asks Beryl. 'Put your hand up.'

'Good grief, I feel that I am in school with a particularly ferocious teacher who I dare not cross!' says Gilbert.

I look around to see if a hand is raised but none have dared. We are all standing or sitting in a large circle in the drawing room and Ralph is shaking his head and refusing to play. I notice the two older women have remained silent. I suspect that Margaret does not support women's suffrage and I know that my wife has no strong feelings about it.

My daughter re-enters the fray with a question: 'Do you not think it incongruous that women in our empire can vote and yet the women of Britain, the country which heads the empire cannot?'

'What women can vote?' asks Erina.

'The women of Canada and Australia.'

'Well, be patient,' says Ralph. 'I expect it will come soon if the suffragettes stop burning Chancellor's houses and smashing up property. Perhaps it is they that have set it all back. Perhaps women behave better in those other countries.'

'It seems silly to me that some women can vote in local elections but not in general elections,' says Beryl abruptly.

'I think it is wrong to deny women a vote when many already hold important positions in society. And how is it right to pay tax but have no say in how things are run?' asks Frances. I see that her initial shyness has evaporated and that she is quite enjoying arguing alongside Beryl. Perhaps they will become friends.

'But who will *do* it for us?' asks Megan and she looks at her father with an impish smile as she speaks.

'Women will have the vote by the time you're grown up my dear,' he says with a short laugh. 'But we can't very well reward violence can we? So it has to wait.'

'Well I think it's got a lot to do with the fact that there are no women in office,' says Beryl, and I feel proud of her. 'No man cares passionately enough to do the job and for that reason, we are stuck.'

'You will get it eventually, when the time is right you know,' says Dei. 'And there are plenty of men who are campaigning for it.

'Eventually. Oh that is not good enough for the women who have campaigned and who will be dead by then.'

'Well you won't get the Tories to take it on,' says Dei after a short silence when no one seems to want to continue. 'They'll give you some nonsense about how giving women the vote will destroy the home but then they might consider titled or propertied women worthy of it. The type that'd vote Conservative of course. The Liberals won't do it because they don't want the Tories to benefit through entitling only elite women and excluding the working class.'

'And some working class men still don't have the vote,' says Tim.

'Then maybe it is a Labour government that we need to take it on,' says Beryl, and she looks at me as she says it.

'The Liberals will do it in time,' I say. 'But Home Rule for Ireland is the biggest headache for the government right now. As my dear friend Tim here will tell you, it's an old problem that has become more intractable over time. Ireland is a country split and possibly on the brink of civil war as we speak, and no, most of the Irish MPs won't support female suffrage. It's not seen as important compared to Home Rule.'

'So when Home Rule goes through, then maybe women will get their vote,' says Beryl.

'It makes sense.'

'When will Home Rule go through though?'

'Oh from one controversy to another. Save us!' I cry.

'Home Rule can go through now thanks to the Parliament Act,' says Dei. 'But the terms are causing problems.'

'And there'll be civil war in Ulster. The Unionists won't accept it,' I say.

Yes, they're a particularly virulent minority,' says Dei. 'And not such great supporters of union with the rest of Great Britain as one might think. Perhaps it would be simpler if it were only that, but as our friend Tim here can tell you, it's more about the interests of the Protestant north against those of the Catholic majority.'

'So much for Christians,' says Ralph and he bangs his stick down. 'There'll be a holy war there in Ireland, mark my words.'

'It might not come to that yet. But I don't think we can go on as we are either, things are getting worse in Ireland and blood will be shed if something doesn't change soon,' says Tim. 'It's true that the Ulster volunteers have armed themselves and vowed to stage a rebellion if Home Rule goes through, and nationalists are just as ready to fight, but I want to believe a settlement can be found.'

'We'll probably end up having two separate Home Rule set ups for the North and the South,' says Dei. 'As I've said before, you need only see one side in a fight, but you need to see both for a settlement.'

'It's a shame more don't think like that,' I say.

'I don't support partitioning as you know,' says Tim. He speaks quietly, but sometimes this is a precursor to one of his polemics. I think it might be time to change the subject.

'Oh I don't care about Irish Home Rule. Better to give it to the Welsh!'

'Beryl, really!' I cry.

'I think the Irish have the campaigning power and the numbers in parliament,' says Dei.

'All I want to know is when women will get the vote. I'm just as clever as Gerald and Mark,' says Beryl.

'She is that,' says Gerald.

'I'll dress as a man if you want. I could be a man instead.'

'Oh my dear don't be silly,' says Selina.

'I'm not. You could cut my hair and I'd borrow some of Gerald's suits. I think Mark's too thin.'

'A hunger strike wouldn't do you too much harm,' says Mark.

'Really, Mark. Don't encourage her.'

At this point Gilbert tells us he has to leave and we say our farewells and it is only after he's gone that I remember our important conversation and I feel quite guilty for not listening to him. I will have to get in touch with him soon, it's important since both of us are close to retirement age. And I will have to apologise to him for my rudeness today. The others are still arguing, though I've not been following.

'—well women deserve some meaning to their lives, more opportunities to work and be useful. Otherwise it all feels a bit pointless,' says Beryl.

'You'll have work enough to do when you have children,' says Selina.

'Yes, don't wish it on yourself,' says Erina.

'Who says I'll have any?'

'You will. I want heirs,' I say.

'Gerald will give you heirs. That's another thing that's unfair; I'm the eldest yet he'll be the one who will be the next Lord Devonport.'

'Well you can't very well be a Lord my dear,' says Selina with a little laugh.

'No. Maybe I won't be a mother either then. It seems to me that if men gave birth it would be quite the racquet. They'd get paid for it since it's such a job after all.'

'Haven't we heard enough now? Let's have some tea before anyone gets really angry,' says Selina.

'There are already a few red faces,' laughs Mark.

'Time for a game,' says Gerald.

The sun has gone behind a cloud and Beryl is standing by an open window; a slight, cool breeze catches at the decorations on her hat. I can see that she's deciding whether or not to carry on, but there's an exhausted energy about the room now. The ruins of our lunch are being digested and I think a cigar and a game of cards will do before afternoon tea. Still, I'm glad the party didn't fall flat. Better a fight and something to remember it by. The ladies will go off now and perhaps continue their topic out of our earshot. I've antagonised my daughter about wanting heirs. She's quite bellicose and I find myself shrinking away from arguing with her at these times. Yet I also admire her, because she has fought well and she is right. I have no disagreement with her on this topic but no great passion for it either. It'll come eventually but can't it wait a bit while we settle other things? I suppose it's an English thing, not wanting too much change too quickly. I see that Frances is less belligerent, yet just as assertive in a more magnanimous way. Such a woman could be an MP herself. But I won't discount my Beryl from that either. There is after all many a man in public life who cannot control his temper and why should women be held to higher standards? Both could serve as well as any man. And little Megan too.

16

Beryl

I have left them to their games, preferring to get away from them all. Ralph and his kind are relics of the past.

It is late afternoon and the air is cooler out on the moor. I follow a sheep path through the heather to the pond that I often visit. I think that it might be a small quarry from which they took slate for the house, but it holds enough water to be a pond and there's something about bodies of water that attracts. Of course it's not as fantastic as the babbling brook that runs hither and thither through a fairy glen of rocks and moss and little waterfalls, but that is a longer walk and I'm in one of my best day dresses. I will miss afternoon tea but I do not care; all we seem to do is eat, and Mark's comment has upset me too. My rounded figure has always been admired, but perhaps if I keep eating all the food they give me, I'll end up as big as Mama. Mark can mock, but he's only slim because he has always been a fussy eater; yet it is he that gets to go to Oxford.

My dress catches on the heather and if it doesn't stop doing that, I'll let it rip. Clothe me in heather instead, purple is one of my colours. I think of my purple room at Gwylfa and turn to look back at the house. Oh it looks glorious in the sun. It shines. At first I didn't like the white paint too much and thought father was being impossible on insisting on it, after all it's a big house and not a little Welsh cottage, but actually it looks rather fantastic. It turns pink at sunset, and it's a beacon in the sun, and on rainy, cloudy days it looks rather grey and forlorn but it never hides like it used to when it was wood. I adore the house and I adore coming here. The air is clear and thin and there is open, uninhabited space. I can see so far from my bedroom window, I see cloud shadows and distant mountains, and sometimes the clouds that roll up look like distant fantasy hills. I love it too when it's misty and you can watch funny drifting wisps of cloud drifting through the valley. The forest in particular breathes out its own clouds, there are forever puffs of air hanging over the pines like steam. Sometimes, I look at the dark pines and wonder what it would be like to go there. While we were on the terrace eating, I was looking at it and thinking of running off. But who can run in a corset?

When I get to the pond, he is there. It's a shock because I didn't expect it. I gave him a note last night, but did I really think he'd come? He stands up and takes off his cap and gives a little bow. Mumbles something that sounds like 'milady'. I laugh and tell him not to bow to me. Today I am just any woman and he is any man. He looks embarrassed and laughs as he looks down at his feet. I have admired those legs. I first saw them when he was bringing the peat in for the fire. He was wearing breeches but for some reason, was barefoot that day. He apologised to me and went on with his work, but I remember his legs, the bone of his knee and the shapely calf.

His name is Owen. Am I a bad woman, to think of a younger man of lower class? He's a grown man, no boy; he must have feelings, like the ones I have. Does he think of me? I have given him enough cause, but he does not show much interest. Still, he is here now.

'My lady—'

'Beryl. Call me Beryl.'

'I—er. I don't think it's proper that I've come. I should be going back.'

'Don't go,' I say. 'Stay a little. Look where we are. We're on the moor and there's only heather and sky.'

'I have work to do,' he says, still holding his cap and looking at me in a reproachful way.

'Oh forget work for a minute,' I say. 'I like to talk to you, but I can't very much, now that we've been forbidden. Ever since that day when you came in to do the fire and we had a little talk, I've enjoyed our conversations.'

'Your father doesn't like it.'

'We're safe here. There's no one to watch us. We don't have to live our lives always for other people. Don't you feel so free being here? Being away from everyone who watches and judges?'

At least he has stopped long enough to listen and now, he is looking at me too. His eyes are light blue, and his hair long at the fringe but short at the back and black as coal. I think of him as my young Celt.

'It's not proper,' he repeats. 'You know I've been warned before. I don't want to lose my job.'

'It's my entire fault,' I say. 'I won't let them dismiss you. Have no fear.'

He shakes his head and looks down.

'Who cares about being proper? Wouldn't you like to travel the world and have adventures? I know I would.'

'I'm always here,' he says. 'I don't really go far from here.'

'Yes, perhaps you working class men have too few rights. Wouldn't you like to vote regardless of whether you own or rent property?'

'My father tells me it makes no difference.'

'Oh I think it does. It's getting better, thanks to the Liberal Party.'

113

'I'm sure you know more than I do, your father being in the government and all that. And I should like the vote, if only to be the same as others.'

'Walk with me,' I say. 'I should like it if you taught me something of your language and of local culture, and in return, I will try to answer any questions you have about the wider world.'

He does not answer so I go on. I walk ahead of him because the path is narrow, but I take every opportunity to look back into his eyes as we talk. 'First, I should like you to tell me of someone famous who is from this area, and what they are famous for.'

He does not look much enamoured with my little game, but I must do something to make him talk to me.

'You may know,' he says after a short silence, 'but there is a statue in Llansannan. Your father paid for it.'

'I remember it. Go on.'

'It carries the names of men from this area who became famous, mostly for writing.'

'I confess to knowing nothing about them.'

'The oldest of them is Tudur Aled on account of him being born in the fifteenth century. He was a bard. We learned about him in school.'

'I am pleased to hear of it,' I say, having stopped and turned towards him. 'Tell me more of this. What is a bard exactly? I have a notion that it is someone who writes poetry and songs.'

Owen nods. 'Yes. They were poets, storytellers and composers. They were paid by a Lord to sing his praises.'

'And if the Lord did not pay?'

'They wrote satires instead.'

'Do you write poems?' I ask.

'I have written some.'

'Oh, I should love to see them.'

'No, that cannot be.'

'Why not?'

'They are not good enough to be seen. I am sure you could do much better.'

'I am sure I could not. I hope that you will trust me enough one day to give me one of your poems. Now, do you have anything you want to ask me about? It is your turn.'

Owen shakes his head and looks back towards the house. I look too. It is small with distance, acres of moor separate us, and above us is a whole kingdom of clouds and sky. I wonder briefly if anyone is looking for us, but brush that thought away.

'I should go back,' he says.

'Five more minutes, please,' I implore him, taking his hand and gripping it tightly. 'Since you won't tell me about your poetry, tell me more about bards and their verses.'

'I don't know very much,' he says. 'Tudur Aled wrote verses called *Cywydd*, it's a kind of Welsh poetry, but you can do them in any language. We wrote some in my final year at school. They have to have seven syllables on each line with rhyming couplets, and more besides. They're quite complicated and there's many kinds.'

I realise I am holding my breath as I watch him talk. 'Oh I love it, Owen,' I say, squeezing his hand. 'How wonderful that the Welsh people have their own special types of poetry.'

'They go in and out of fashion.'

'But perhaps at the Eisteddfod they are still performed?'

'Yes, there maybe.'

I laugh. 'I am quite surprised.'

'At what?'

'That you know all this.'

'Do you think me a fool?' He sounds disappointed, rather than angry.

'Forgive me,' I say. 'I can see that you are an intelligent man, and that it is foolish to think that only people with money are clever, when often they are not. You have a certain way about you that I admire very much, but you are quiet and humble. You do not sing your own praises.'

'Can you hear that?' he says, looking away from me, towards the distant sound of a bird calling.

'Yes, what is it?'

'It's a Golden Plover. They come here in the summer to breed. You'll see them on the coast in winter though.'

'It makes a mournful sound. It makes me feel quite sad,' I say, stopping and looking at him. 'Are you happy Owen?'

He gives me a half smile. 'I'm happy enough.'

I reach out my hand to touch his cheek. His skin is soft, except for where the hair is trying to grow back through. There it rasps. I touch his lips. Finely sculpted they are, like those Ancient Greeks whose anatomy I have marvelled at in museums. He still looks reproachful and I imagine he feels as I did when one of my father's business friends cornered me, thinking no one was looking. I lower my hand, not liking that I feel like the predator, but he surprises me by suddenly taking my hand and kissing me quickly on the cheek.

'I have to go now,' he says and replaces his cap.

'Don't go yet,' I grab his arm in a most unladylike way. I am not quite sure what has come over me but I return his kiss, most impulsively on his mouth and it hurts my lips, the force of it. But at least he looks at me a little differently now. His expression is softer as if he has overcome his fear.

My insides jump as I feel his lips touch my cheek and my hands go around his waist, seemingly of their own accord as if they have known how to do this all along. I pull him closer and he puts his hands around my face, his fingertips touching my ears and the earrings that dangle there. He brings his face close and looks at me for a moment before kissing me properly on the lips. I want the kiss to stretch on and on, yet I can hardly breathe inside my corset and feel as if I might pass out at any moment.

I grip his arm, feeling the roundness and hardness of the muscle. He laughs in a self-conscious way.

'Am I just a plaything to you?' he asks.

'No, I'm quite serious about you. I've been after you for years. You know this. Please believe me.'

'I'd be dismissed if they caught us like this,' he says, looking down at me. 'Your father has a telescope on the roof.'

'Stop worrying, I will not let them dismiss you.' I keep my arms tight around him, because I don't want him to go yet. 'Lie down with me in the heather. It's safer, then no one will see us, including father with his confounded telescope.'

He follows my lead, laying down and propping himself up on an elbow. He looks at me, as I lie back on a bed of heather.

'When I go to parties, I find myself looking for you,' I say. 'Sometimes I might see a man, who has something of you in him. Maybe it's his dark hair or his height, or his blue eyes; but I'm always disappointed that it's not you.'

He laughs and I think he looks happy. His eyes are shining and I can see that he is still quite in awe of me.

'Lie with me,' I say. 'And hold me.'

I feel muscle, bone, and his arms taut around me. Lying against him, I look at the sky and laugh.

17

Gwen

March 1954

'I found this in my bedroom,' says Dewi.

He has barged into my room like an elephant, but I'll forgive him.

'What is it?' I ask.

'It's a photograph,' he says, sitting next to me on the bed, and holding it so I can see. When I try to take it, he won't let me.

'Let me see it properly,' I say, pulling it from his fingers.

'Careful Gwen! You'll rip it.'

I see an old picture of a girl who I'm beginning to think I know well, although her hair is different, it's the first time I've seen it all let down; long, dark and wavy. She's smiling like she is very happy and she wears a hat with a ribbon and a frilly ivory-coloured dress. The photograph is clearly old and a bit tatty. I turn it round and there are dirty fingerprints on the back.

'Where did you find this?' I ask.

'It's her isn't it?' says Dewi. 'The one in the paintings.'

'Yes, but where did you get it?'

'It was strange when I come to think of it,' says Dewi. 'There are cracks all round my window, that let draughts in and I've been seeing it for a while, but I didn't think anything of it.'

'What?'

'I could just see the edge of it. Someone must have pushed it into the crack between the window frame and the wall. I've been looking at the edge of it for ages, only today I thought, what is that? I got it out with Mam's tweezers.'

'I hope you put them back, we're in enough trouble as it is.'

'Why would it be there?' says Dewi.

'I don't know. Maybe someone stole it and hid it. One of the servants.'

'Why would anyone do that?'

'Maybe one of the servants was in love with her.'

Dewi pretends to vomit.

'I bet one of the servants took the photograph because they wanted to do voodoo on her,' says Dewi.

'Keep the picture hidden,' I say. 'Otherwise Mam will take it.'

'You have it,' says Dewi and hands it to me.

*

It's a relief now that Mam and Tad are looking with us, even if they've wasted an hour looking everywhere that we've already tried. We didn't admit to leaving Alis behind on purpose though. They know nothing about that.

They've gone out onto the moor now and if they don't find her there, they'll call the police. Mam's last words to us: 'You two have got some explaining to do. You should have told us as soon as you knew she was missing.' Tad just looked really mad but didn't say a thing. Turmoil. That's what we're in now. Dewi has been trying to get a story straight with me. He's ever the one to lie and weasel his way out of things, he just doesn't like being in trouble.

'We're in trouble and that's that,' I told him. 'We have to face the music.'

I got that from my teacher. When someone stole the rubber off her desk, she encouraged them to own up and then gave us all a lecture on facing the music of our actions. We would be better people for it. But Dewi still wants to lie.

'Well,' I say to the silent room. 'We should make sure our story is close to the truth at least. It's easier to lie if it's only a little one.'

'Yes,' Dewi agrees. 'I thought we could say that Alis asked us to leave her in the chest.'

I laugh. 'Why would she do that?'

'I don't know. You're a girl, you tell me.'

'A girl is a person just like you are.'

We're sitting in the playroom, which is one of the servant's bedrooms that has no bed and we've made it into a games room. We put toys, games and books in here that we don't mind sharing. Of course, Dewi's comics are all in his room and I don't bring my Britains animal figures in here or my red Massey Ferguson tractor. And Alis doesn't have any of her junk in here because she hoards everything under her bed.

I'm drawing little pictures of Alis in my sketchbook. In one she's being eaten by a monster that looks like a crocodile. In another she's fallen down a deep well with black water at the bottom. I'm on my third now, in this one she's stuck in the chimney. I suppose I should stop in case one of them comes true. We'll have to think of a story soon, or Mam and Tad will be back and we'll be in big trouble. It's not as if they don't know that we bully Alis a bit.

Dewi must have been thinking along the same lines: 'What if we say that Alis was trying to shut you in the box and then she said it was her turn, and she told us to go back because she was braver than us and could go back all by herself. And she called us chickens because we thought it was a bad idea.'

120

'Hmm. Not your best one Dewi, but not your worst either. Trouble is you know Alis won't corroborate your story.'

'Corr—what?'

'Cor-ro-bor-rate,' I say it slowly. It's another new word, but not the easiest to say, maybe I'll ditch it.

'She won't agree with your story.'

'So what?' says Dewi. 'It's two against one.'

'And they will believe who?'

'Her probably,' says Dewi resignedly. 'Might be better if she stays lost, then we can say whatever we want.'

'That's a terrible thing to say!'

'Well it's true. Don't tell me you haven't thought it yourself.'

'No, I have not!'

But I have, and Dewi's right, we're a pair of awful cowards that don't want our parents to be mad with us.

Dewi starts looking at a book, while I go to the window to look for our parents. There are lots of footprints in the snow, but no sign of them.

'They're taking ages. Don't you think it's a bit weird?' I ask.

Dewi looks up and for a brief moment, I feel sad that he's suffering. His face looks tense and even paler than usual.

'What's weird?' he asks.

'Well, the way she's just disappeared.'

'Yeah, I've been trying to work out where she would go. To think like her. But I can't think of anything.'

'Maybe someone took her away.'

'Who would come up here in all this snow?'

'I don't know,' I say. 'But when I was in the kitchen with Tad, I thought I saw something pass the window.'

'You're always seeing things.'

'Hey!'

'We still need to get our story straight,' says Dewi.

We lapse into another silence and I start tidying toys onto the shelves. This room doesn't have much furniture, but it has tall shelves and an old chest of drawers with a tarnished mirror. I look at myself and think I look washed out, even my freckles have gone pale.

'I have an idea,' I say.

'Not another one,' groans Dewi.

'Listen,' I say firmly because an important word has popped into my head. Confidence. That's what we need.

'We could say, she went to bed like normal last night and then give some of the guilt to Mam and Tad by asking them, in our most innocent voices: how was she when you checked in on her? I mean they always used to check in on us didn't they?'

'Ah, yes,' says Dewi. 'Not bad. I can't even remember when they stopped checking on us.' He fiddles with a soldier that's lying on the floor near him and I notice that it's one of the little metal ones that he used to keep in a tin under his pillow. Not so precious now it seems. As I look around the room, I see them everywhere as if he just opened the tin and threw them all over the room. Knowing Dewi, that wouldn't surprise me.

'I suppose we still have the same problem though. I mean if she says that isn't true,' says Dewi.

'It's a simple enough lie to tell. We just say we were sure she went to bed. And then we say, oh but, maybe she sleepwalked back into the other-house.'

'But Mam and Tad will question us about how we thought she got back. Did she follow us, were we with her?' says Dewi.

'Yes and we just have to be sure sounding in our lie. We can't say, oh she might have been, or we think she was there.

We have to say she was *definitely* with us. And even if they find her and she's denying it, we have to say but you've forgotten, Alis, you were with us. We have to be sure, Dewi. No one can crack us. It's just one lie and it's half true anyway.'

'Is it?'

'Yes, because we both kept thinking and saying that she was probably back in her room last night. So it's like a half-lie.'

'I see. If we are really sure in our lie, we can make Mam and Tad believe us and even Alis will have to believe us and maybe she'll start to think she's mad and she's remembered it all wrong. Mam and Tad already think she's a bit mad anyway.'

'That's it.'

Dewi laughs. 'Look at this. Do you remember it?' He holds up the book he's reading.

I laugh. 'Let's do it again.'

Once again I give Dewi one of my long skirts and I wear the other. We can only find one of the plastic moustaches though so I use some of Mam's eyeliner to draw the moustache on my face.

'I wish we had hats though,' I say. 'Bowler hats like in the book.'

'Yes and you need to tie your hair back to make it harder for people to know if you're a boy or a girl.'

'Or both,' I say. 'Let's put woolly hats on, they'll do.'

I plait my hair and tuck it into my jumper. We look in the bathroom mirror and laugh at our work, then prance around the house talking in strange mannish voices, because our top half is a man. And we skip because our bottom half is a woman. Last time we did this, we posed like the illustration in the book, with me sitting on a chair and Dewi standing behind me. Mam thought it was so funny that she used the Polaroid to take a photograph of us.

'Let's go into the other-house like this,' I say. 'Maybe we can find her before they get back and we look like investigators.'

'Do we?' says Dewi, wiggling his moustache. 'I thought we looked like man-ladies.'

'M'ladies,' I say.

*

We hold our breath for a few seconds as we open the chest, but of course she hasn't magically reappeared in there. Yet I still believe in magic, if that makes me a baby, then so be it. After that I lead Dewi down to the dining room with the portraits, still skipping.

'Tad has forgotten to take them down,' I say. 'Maybe I'll tell him I had another nightmare.'

'What are you on about?' says Dewi irritably.

'I've had an idea.'

'Is there ever going to be an end to your ideas?'

'Shush. If our parents are really mad with us and keep on being mad, we just have to start having a lot of nightmares and doing crazy things like sleepwalking.'

'You mean we turn into Alis.'

I laugh. 'In a way. But if we act all nervous, as if it's affected us badly, they will feel bad about staying mad at us.'

'You call me sneaky, but listen to you,' says Dewi.

I point at the picture of Selina up on the wall. 'I told Tad that she gives me nightmares.'

'She does look a bit strict.'

'Which one is her husband?'

Dewi shrugs.

'I think it's that one,' I say. 'Lord Devonport.'

Dewi regards the portrait and I'm guessing that he hasn't ever looked at them closely before; not like I do.

'What are you thinking?' I ask.

'Wait,' he says. 'I'm getting something on him.' Dewi wiggles his fingers and sways side to side like a mad person. 'Yes, I'm getting something. Okay, here's his story—he comes back here at night. It was his house first and he wants it back.'

'Tad says he's dead Dewi.'

'Even better. Ghosts can just fly back here. Just like that. And he sits in his old chair like he used to when he was alive and he flicks prunes at his guests using his silver spoons. His guests have come back as ghosts too. He invited them to a ghost party here. And he goes up to sleep his old bedroom but wakes in the night to the jabbering ghost of his father sitting on the end of his bed.'

'A ghost haunting a ghost,' I say. 'Never heard of such a thing. And that's from *The Listing Attic* again. I know you copied it.'

'I added some of my own details,' says Dewi.

'What about him them?' I point at Gerald's portrait.

'He lures children to a dark copse and then beats them to death with his cane.'

'He doesn't have a cane,' I say. 'He's too young and handsome.'

Dewi laughs. 'You love him.'

'No, I don't. Anyway, he'll be an old man now, so perhaps you're right.'

'And here is the wicked daughter, Beryl.'

'Oh no. She's not wicked, she's the innocent one. Like Cinderella. And you are going to save her and marry her.'

'What an old woman? No thanks. I'm not marrying anyone.'

'Well neither am I. I think those white dresses look silly.'

'You can marry Lloyd George,' says Dewi.

I look at the picture of Lloyd George, which is alone and on a different wall.

'I'm not sure if I want to,' I say. 'Is he even alive anymore?'

'You'll be very unhappy in your marriage and you will throw yourself under a carriage.'

'I know you got that from the book,' I say. 'Now him,' I point at Mark Kearley.

'Wears a hair shirt, eats dirt and bathes in brine.'

'Oh. What's brine?'

'Salty water,' says Dewi. 'Did you hear that?'

'What?'

'I thought I heard a noise.'

'No. What kind of noise?'

'Like a door shutting somewhere in the house.'

'Oh heck. Maybe Mam and Tad are back. Maybe they've found her.'

We stand stock still and look at each other as we listen. I realise that it probably doesn't look good that we're wearing moustaches and skirts. But all thoughts of fixing that disappear as I hear what Dewi heard. There's a shuffling sound and then a moaning. I find myself gripping Dewi's sleeve and he doesn't even tell me to get off. Trepidation. It's the best word I know for scared in anticipation of something.

'Is it a ghost?' I whisper.

Dewi looks sideways at me and puts a finger to his lips.

'No, I think it's Alis,' he says.

18

When Alis walks into the dining room, I think at first that she is actually dead like in my drawings and has come back as a ghost. And there's an awful smell. It's a lot to take in. She's naked except for the black bracelet and her bobble hat. Most of her top half is filthy with what appears to be soot, but there's something else too. There's brown stuff on her. A lot of it, down her legs and up her back.

We should be glad to see her, but I notice that Dewi is looking at her in disgust. Then he pinches his nose.

'Hell, you stink,' he says and turns to me, 'she's pooed herself.'

Alis whimpers. I can't quite make out any words. She stands at the door with her dirty black hands extended towards us. I have mixed feelings, relief and disgust, and could it be disappointment?

'Where have you been?' I say in a voice that sounds commanding and cold.

'I don't know,' Alis says and bursts into tears.

Dewi and I look at each other. I think we both know what the other is thinking.

'Mam and Tad are looking for you,' I say. 'If they see you like that, you'll be in big trouble.'

Alis cries and walks towards us.

How did you get all that filth on you?

Alis's crying turns into a frown with her chin jutting out. 'You did this.'

'Don't blame us, we didn't make you poo,' says Dewi.

'You locked me in.'

'Locked?' I say. 'No one locked anything.'

'You did,' she starts crying again and I half wish she would just disappear and stay missing, but that's mixed with guilt.

'We'll have to get her cleaned up Dewi,' I say, in a loud, confident voice, which is put on of course. 'Before our parents see her. Then they won't be mad.'

'I'm not touching her or her poo,' says Dewi, grimacing.

'Go and get some clothes for her,' I say. 'Alis, stop being such a baby. You need to get the worst of it off yourself or I won't help you. You're old enough to clean yourself up really.'

'Good luck with that,' says Dewi.

'Take your hat off and put it in the wash.'

'Nooo,' she whinges.

'You have to. It's full of soot.'

I pull it off her head. I know she is attached to it because it was the last thing Nain knitted before she passed away. Alis was close to our grandmother.

'Come on,' I say. 'Let's go into the toilet. I'll run the bath. You wipe yourself.'

Once I get her into the bath, she stops crying, but still smells awful because a lot of it is dried on and wetting it makes the stink worse, so I open the window. I marvel at the state of her. She looks as if she has had an accident in her pants, then taken them off and gone up the chimney.

'Where did you go after we all went to bed?' I ask. And before she can answer, I do it for her. 'Sleep-walking again were you? You've caused us all a lot of worry. Mam and Tad are out looking for you now. They could be back at any minute.'

Alis starts crying again. 'It's cold,' she whimpers, looking round at the open window. She is hunched over in the water and I can see her spine sticking out through her skin.

'You haven't answered my question,' I say. 'Where did you go?'

'You left me.'

'What are you on about? We all went back together. I hope you're not going to lie to Mam and Tad after I've helped you like this. It's going to take a lot of cleaning to get you right and then after you get out, I'll have to get this bath clean again.'

'You left me in the chest.'

The smell and the mess she's making is getting right up my nose and making me angry. I want to smack her and then *slap*. I do it, without really planning to. She starts up crying again, only louder and sort of bad-tempered sounding. I regret hitting her of course. There's my hand mark all red on her back. Better hope she doesn't see it. Or Mam and Tad. With a new sense of urgency, I sponge her all over and tell her to pull the plug out as Dewi appears at the door with clothes.

'Dewi, get me a towel please. One of the brown ones.'

He goes off again and I refill the bath while she's still crouching there.

'Ow, it's too hot,' she says, standing up.

So I put the cold on full.

'Ahhh, too cold.'

'Stop moaning,' I say. 'You said you don't remember where you've been. You must have been sleep-walking then Alis. Or else you've gone mad. We definitely didn't leave you in the other-house. We most *definitely* did not.'

I say it with confidence and with a harsh edge to my voice. I'm just letting her know who is boss.

She's looking cleaner now, but when I look at the plug hole I feel angry again, although I stop myself from smacking her. The red mark on her back is fading to pink and doesn't look like a hand anymore.

'There you go,' I say. 'You're clean enough. There's still a bit of a whiff, but I think it'll take a few baths to get back to normal.'

Dewi hands me a towel.

'Now go and find Mam and Tad,' I tell him, marvelling at how bossy I sound. 'But take that skirt off first for heaven's sake.'

'We were told to stay here,' he argues.

'You don't have to go far. Just go outside the door and shout for them.'

He disappears, and I rub Alis's hair with the brown towel.

'When you're dry get dressed,' I tell her. 'You can do that yourself. Then use the soap and wash your face, there's still black round your eyes. And then you'll be as good as new.' I wrinkle my nose. 'Well almost. Put that towel in the wash and no one will ever know.'

In the end, I can't leave her in case she disappears again so I help dress her and start to be a bit nicer now I'm not being made angry by that awful smell.

'Put some talc on,' I say. 'It'll make you smell better and I'll lend you a bit of my perfume.'

She's still hiccupping and sniffing from all that crying, but I can tell she's starting to recover.

'I'm so glad we found you,' I say. 'We were worried. We've been looking everywhere for you. Dewi and I wanted to find you to surprise Mam and Tad. Now we can all be a happy family again.'

She doesn't say anything but carries on sniffing. She's traumatised of course.

'I'll let you play with my dolls if you like,' I say. I know how much she has dearly wished for that, but she may be too upset to care. She's still shivering so I close the window.

'Come and sit by the fire in the kitchen now,' I say. 'That'll get you warm again and I'll get you a drink too. Are you hungry?'

She whimpers a few words here and there, but my attempts to get her on my side are failing. It feels like she's bottling things up and waiting, just waiting to tell on Dewi and me when Mam and Tad get back. I hope Dewi remembers our agreed story. At least her hair is so curly that it doesn't get properly wet, it'll soon be dry now she's by the fire. There's still some tiny black dots on her scalp but I'd never be able to get it all out in one go.

'I'll just quickly clean the bath,' I say. 'We don't want them to work out what you did. Now don't go anywhere and just shout if you want something.'

I wait for an answer, but all she gives is a little nod.

19

Hudson

June 1917

We are a reduced party this summer. The war that came was bloody but not as quick as they predicted, as if they knew what it would be like. It may seem illogical that Europe should plunge itself willingly into such horror and hardship, and to keep going at it when it is clear that to continue is only to heap on more pointless suffering; but the pride and stupidity of men knows no bounds. Though I am too old to be on the front, I have done my part at home and suffered many anxieties while waiting to hear from my boy Mark who was backpacking with his friend in Germany in the summer of 1914. He wasn't alone, when war broke out, many people, those high in office included, were abroad and out of place; a testament to how it was not expected until it happened. It is now three years since we last saw Mark.

Just a month before it all began I recall dining with Admiral Jellicoe and his wife, and at the time, they accepted an invitation to stay at Gwylfa with us for the shoot in September. I made a joke about a war possibly ruining our plans and we laughed. A few weeks later, he was off to take up his position in command of the Grand Fleet and we didn't end up visiting Gwylfa at all that year.

As well as worrying about Mark abroad in Germany, my older son Gerald was seriously ill and when he recovered he joined the fighting. We are in the third year of it and I have heard much from Dei of his frustrations with the formality and lethargy of the officials at the War Office. He felt that his first fight was against them, and the stubbornness of characters such as Kitchener, led him to complain that the war would be lost by old men desperately clinging onto power. He was eventually successful in gaining permission to create a committee for arms production, after alarming reports of shortages from the front. Though a pacifist, Dei became passionate when he saw that involvement in the war was difficult to avoid after the invasion of neutral Belgium. He was always one to fight for the underdog.

During these years, the Tories have warmed to him and relations with the more pacifist Liberals and Labour have cooled somewhat, such is the voracity of his involvement. At first he took a lower job in a role created for the war, Minister for Munitions, but as the war has dragged on, it is clear that my old friend Asquith is not a war leader and he was replaced with Lloyd George in 1916. It was Northcliffe's meddling that arguably brought about the event of Asquith's fall, though perhaps it was inevitable.

There has been some dismay at the inadequate living conditions for the poorest of this country that have conspired to produce men too weak to fight and the heavy drinking is a problem for a nation where the pubs never close. Dei has fought to improve both areas, with some success although he failed to get breweries nationalised. I begin to see that the German system of social welfare has served them well. For my part, I have been back in office, doing what I can, though I am not the man I was.

I am here at my writing desk, thinking these painful thoughts, when Beryl enters the room. I look up at her with what I suppose must have been a frown because she looks to her mother with a question.

'Have you heard anything more about the boys?' she asks.

Selina is here in the library with me, quietly reading the papers on the chaise longue.

'Nothing on Gerald. Mark's still at Ruhleben as far as we know,' Selina answers.

'I blame Northcliffe for this,' I say, swinging my chair round to face them. My anger is ever ready to spring out when certain subjects are brought up. 'His stupid sensationalism demanding that all Germans on our soil be taken prisoner caused their retaliation without a doubt, it's criminal; until then Mark had a chance of coming home. If he couldn't have come home he could have stayed with Lady Herkomer. Now, who knows how long it'll be.'

'They'll keep him prisoner until it's over,' says Beryl with a sigh.

'I expect so,' replies Selina.

'When's Ralph arriving?' I ask, wanting to change the subject. 'Haven't seen the old fellow in a year.'

'He's due any time,' says Selina with a roll of her eyes. 'And God help us.'

*

My friend Ralph can be difficult and somewhat old-fashioned in his views but I find him rather entertaining and I know that Beryl does too, despite their disagreements.

We are taking afternoon tea in the library as we've gotten rather comfortable there. The food is not lavish, but adequate. We have a few simple cakes and a pot of tea and are as contented with that as we were once with plates and plates of sandwiches, cold meats, fancies, and pots of clotted cream.

I watch Ralph insert a whole cake into his mouth with ease, but then they are quite small. Still we are not rationing yet, at least not officially, despite my efforts the government has been reluctant. We are merely taking part in voluntary rationing for the time being. I've no doubt it'll be compulsory soon and all my hard work in that area will be claimed by another.

'And what's with the job change?' asks Ralph. 'The Welsh Wizard's coup d'état was all over the papers, but I didn't know you were back in politics and as soon as you're back in, you're out again.'

I groan. 'Must I tell this tale again?'

'He had to resign due to ill health,' says Selina. 'The doctor wrote most forcibly that he would suffer a breakdown and permanent health issues. But with rest he can recover.'

'*He* can speak for himself, my dear,' I say. 'Although on this occasion I am tempted to let you tell the tale as I know you will do it with great detail and loyalty, as well as I ever could.'

'One of you must tell me what happened,' says Ralph. 'For your old friend has heard critical reports from the *The Times* and *The Daily Mail.*'

'That's a polite way of saying they excoriated me.' I pause and look out at the misty hills and wonder if I wouldn't rather just get up and walk out. Get some air. That is why I came here. To recover, not to relive.

'There is not a lot to tell, so I'll be brief,' I say at last. 'When Dei became Prime Minister, I was naïve enough to think it wouldn't affect me. However, a telegram arrived at Wittington in December asking me to meet him at the War Office that evening. I took the train to London and I can tell you, I did it with reluctance. I suppose it never occurred to Dei that I might not want to return to office.'

'He made you an offer?'

'No, he gave a command. He wasted no time in saying that he was setting up a Ministry for Food and that he wanted me to run it. I told him I had enough to do with the Port of

London, which if you remember, I also set up from scratch in more youthful and exuberant days, and it has been good honest work. But to do it all over again? No, I didn't want to, but Lloyd George was insistent. He said he would pass a bill to conscript me if he had to and that I would be creating this new ministry. Everyone must do their part for the war effort, he said.'

'You were in the cabinet?'

'No. There is no cabinet as such at present, only a small war cabinet of four or five, created to wrest control from the War Office, but that's a whole other story. Anyway, I got him to agree that I would be solely in charge. But it has been a headache, Ralph. Once again, I have been tasked with setting up a new department and it has caused me much anxiety, I can tell you, from day one. And if you read the papers, which you clearly do, well, they know what I am about to do before I know myself. There was a journalist here only yesterday. Yes! They even pursued me here as I try to get some peace.'

Now that I am telling the story, I see it is running away with me and my wife is watching me with an anxious look. Too late, I must tell it as well as I can.

'To give Northcliffe his due, he did offer help in getting the right men for my department in the beginning. I wanted business minded men rather than civil servants, you see. Since then, he seems to have developed a hatred for me. I am not sure what changed. Perhaps I do not have such winning ways with journalists. Perhaps I should have learned to keep them buttered up. Anyway, I won't go on.'

'But what exactly do you do there?' asks Ralph. 'It's important work I'm sure, but I often wonder what you politicians do all day.'

'I'm not there any longer but my department studied the technical aspects of rationing as well as the likely effects on the people. We presented memorandums which no one read. Does that sound unduly bitter? Well, I was called to conference just last month and Dei, along with his war cabinet, asked me what I had. I asked them in turn if they'd read my memo from three weeks back which had detailed all the findings of my department's detailed study. Clearly no one had bothered to read the thing. Of course, Dei is never at a loss. He immediately tasked some men with conferring with me. The upshot is that my suggestion that we begin compulsory rationing was rejected by the war cabinet. What could I do? I can only advise. But it's galling as I leave my post, almost as reluctantly as I began it, for I like to see my work through and done well. The papers don't care for my story, they have let their cannons loose on me; it's particularly frustrating that Northcliffe knows the truth but chooses to print lies.'

'It's so unfair on Papa,' says Beryl angrily. 'He has worked extremely hard in setting up that Ministry and they accuse him of purposely delaying rationing to protect retailers.'

'Yes, she's right,' I say. 'It's a thankless task, and it is rather annoying that my successor, Rhonddfa is having an easier time of it. But that's politics.'

'And what's the reason for not having compulsory rationing?' asks Ralph, sitting cross-legged in the chair by the fire, stroking his moustache. 'Seems to me there are plenty of fat people who could do with tightening their belts. Especially in London. Last time I was there, in 1913, some awful overweight suffragette was shouting nonsense in the street. All I wanted was to get to the jam and pickle shop.'

I notice Ralph glances briefly at Beryl as he says this. She makes a groaning noise but looks out of the window and doesn't rise to it.

'The government felt that the voluntary rationing was working well,' I say. 'I have to give credit to the royals who themselves adopted it and encouraged the nation to follow. And though things are tight, we didn't want to let the Germans know their submarine campaign was working.'

'And Lloyd George felt that rationing would be unpopular with the people,' says Selina. 'We don't read the *New Statesman*, but they have been whipping up stories about the hardships of life under rations.'

'Yes, yes,' I say. 'And yet even Northcliffe's press had to admit that the rationing scheme I proposed was more generous than those of some other European countries.'

'Life is unfair,' says Beryl, and she looks to her left out of the window, across the moor and I wonder at how she came to look as pale and sad as she does in that high-backed chair by the fire. She is looking thinner about the face too.

'Of course, as soon as the papers begin their attacks, the government is falling over itself trying to do something, but mostly pointing the finger at some scapegoat. If there were an honest politician, he'd be so unusual he'd probably have a halo.'

'Don't upset yourself,' says Selina. 'Have more cake, dear. You've barely touched your tea.'

Normally she wouldn't fuss because she knows I'd tell her to stop, but a man over sixty doesn't have the virulence of youth and I have suffered with more illness than ever before since taking the Food Ministry job. It's my age I suppose, coupled with the fact that my heart was never in it. I pick up my tea cup, feeling oddly emotional.

'Sounds like a job for a saint,' says Ralph, laughing into his teacup, cake crumbs on his moustache. I watch him and wonder at what's funny, and why doesn't he trim that moustache? It's quite out of control.

'I'll be glad when this damn war is over.'

'Beryl, really!' cries Selina in that high, exasperated tone we rarely hear, and yet we've been hearing it more lately. Poor woman has to deal with worries about both of our sons, me complaining about the Food Ministry, and Beryl's depressed state since her fiancé went off to fight.

Dullness settles on us as we sit in the library looking at the fire as our maid Ann puts more peat on it. The dark-haired boy who used to do it has gone to fight too and there is no news of him either. Our staff is very reduced but we appear to manage just as well. Outside, it's a day of cloud and drizzle and a disappearing moor. I would have liked to be on the terrace in the sun, which is how I pictured it when we escaped London and the howling headlines that followed in my wake. I thought I would be holding a glass of something amber-coloured with the incredible climbing song of skylarks and aerobatics of swallows around me, and the bees in the heather, but today is a day for silhouettes in the mist and armchairs by the fire.

'Who could that be?' says Beryl, once again looking out of the windows.

I stand and wonder. A figure approaches but is a mere will-o'-the-wisp in the low, wet cloud that obscures.

'Fiddlesticks,' I say. 'It had better not be another journalist.'

'Shall I get one of your guns?' says Ralph, rising from his chair with some difficulty.

I shake my head. 'Don't tempt me.'

Many possibilities pass through my mind that are not really possibilities at all. First, I imagine that Mark approaches, though I know that he is in prison, and then I see Gerald, which is more likely, although I am not expecting him to be on leave just now, and then I see that our visitor has a stick and is probably quite elderly. He approaches Gwylfa with what appears to be tiredness and relief.

'He looks in need of refreshment, whoever he is,' I say.

'Perhaps he is lost,' says Beryl.

Disappointed that it is not one of our own, but glad of some distraction from our gloom, we all go to the door where one of the maids is acting as footman. I hear the man introducing himself as the Vicar of Rhosgwalia and asking about what sort of food we serve at this inn.

'Inn?' says Ralph. 'You'd better put him right. Silly man is lost. He needs directions to The Sportsman's.'

'No, no,' whispers Beryl. 'Can we play along?'

I look at my wife and she laughs, then nods. 'Why not?' she says. 'It might be a hoot.'

'I'll be in the drawing room with Ralph,' I say.

With the maid's help in the kitchen, the two ladies serve the vicar a hearty meal of cold meats, curried egg, and rhubarb with clotted cream. It's an echo of life before the war, all thoughts of rationing are put aside, and Ralph and I decide to order some too, though this elicits a dark frown from Beryl.

'Abominable service in this place,' says Ralph, puffing on his pipe.

The vicar is bemused and looks from one to the other.

'I think that the service is the best I have ever received at any establishment and that there is no need to be rude to the staff.'

Beryl and Selina begin by smiling but cannot subdue their laughter. Soon they are laughing in a quite undignified way and I see that no amount of Swiss schooling will ever remove that hint of wildness that Beryl has.

The poor vicar is quite perplexed. I think it is time to explain.

'I am sorry, I think we have had quite the joke at your expense,' I say. 'This is not The Sportsman's Arms at all. That is a little further, over the hill and down. I am the owner so I can vouch it serves a good meal and ale if you care for it.'

'Oh dear!' says the vicar. 'Then where on earth am I?'

'Gwylfa Hiraethog,' I say. 'Though do not worry, we have enjoyed having you as our guest.'

'Yes, indeed we have,' says Selina. 'You have quite cheered us on a gloomy day.'

Despite our attempts to soothe him, the poor man has turned crimson.

'May I ask who I have inconvenienced?' he says, standing up.

'It was no inconvenience,' says Selina.

'Lord and Lady Devonport,' says Beryl. 'And I'm their daughter. Ralph—well I haven't a clue where he went—is an old friend of my father's.'

'My Lord and Lady, forgive me.'

'There is no forgiveness needed, in fact we hope that you will forgive us for playing a little trick for our own amusement,' I say.

'Oh yes, yes,' says the vicar, still quite crimson and sweating now too.

'Would you stay for a nip of whisky?' I say. 'I would enjoy talking with you. My friend Ralph will be along in a minute I'm sure, he's probably just gone to the toilet.'

'Well if I am not being a trouble to you,' says the vicar, wiping his chin with his napkin and adjusting his spectacles. 'I would enjoy that.'

20

Beryl

I leave my father with the vicar, they're talking about the war. Everyone here talks about the war and Lloyd George, the two are interchangeable. I can predict the next topic will be Gerald and Mark, that would probably have been the first, but the vicar specifically made a reference to Lloyd George's speech back in 1908. He wanted to know about it. I feel better after our little prank, but I know it won't last. Most days I feel as if I'm in limbo.

I touch my fingertips to the embossed wallpaper in the hallway and laugh a little inside when I remember the feelings I had for Lloyd George and how I thought there was some slight understanding between us. I can almost feel a shameful blush coming on when I remember how I left my bedroom door open and lay waiting for him on my bed in the dark. What a fool I was; with his wife in the house too! I had a lot of strong feelings when I was younger and no one to tell. Nine years later and much to the relief of my parents, I'm engaged. But my passions do still take me sometimes.

Of course, we know now that Lloyd George has been having an affair with his secretary for years, and she's younger than I am. Frances is very clever and is the first woman to have such a high ranking role in the government. I like her, but we all guessed about the affair when he brought her here before the war. He was always having affairs, but then a lot of them were. Papa said they didn't put it in the papers because there's an unofficial code of conduct concerning affairs, and because Northcliffe had several mistresses of his own and a good few illegitimate children. Divorce is another thing entirely, that will always make the papers. What a hypocritical world we live in. Even that old man Asquith was chasing after his daughter's friend, they say that is the reason why he was distracted from his job during the war.

Before and after my brief flirtation with the Chancellor, there was the Celt. His name was Owen, but in my head he was always more fantasy than reality. I never met a man more beautiful and yet, modest with it. I wrote to him a few times over the years, but he never wrote back and the years slipped by without so much as a word. Even so, I had desperately hoped that he would be on leave when we arrived here, but his father told us he is at Ypres in Flanders. My fiancé is there too, but as an officer. I wonder if they will meet. My fiancé Jonathan was the first man I danced with who liked me as much as I liked him. Since Mama and Papa approved of him and I'm going to be thirty soon, I thought he would have to do. But that is perhaps a decision I made rashly and it has caused me some pain, for a part of me has always loved Owen.

Jonathan is a good man. He is not very handsome, but he is tall and kind, with reddish hair and long fingers. He plays the piano well and likes shooting, so Mama and Papa both like him. His family are new wealth, as we are, and there aren't too many airs and graces. I have come to adore them all very much.

The varnished wood of the banister is smooth under my palm as I walk up the stairs. The wallpaper here is a deep plum-coloured botanical. In late summer, it complements the colours outside, but today it's only May and everything is wet and grey. I look out for more silhouettes, Jonathan maybe. No, he wouldn't come here, so I allow myself to think of Owen and our trysts in the heather. He never had much to say and was a secretive sort, which was good because I always feared he would tell. I became highly sensitive if any of the staff laughed when I was around, began turning on them and asking them, what are you laughing at? Do tell. But I don't think he ever told. My maid Dora, was the only one who knew.

As I walk upstairs, Ralph is coming down, labouring with his walking stick.

'You could use the downstairs cloakroom,' I say as I watch him pause for breath.

'No thank you,' he says. 'I prefer the wallpaper up here.'

I turn as he passes, his breath rasping. Ralph has always been old to me, but I'm shocked at how decrepit he has become. I walk up slowly, watching until he reaches the bottom to make sure he doesn't fall, but he manages it. He will go off for a glass of whisky with Papa and the vicar now. I hope that makes him feel happy.

My room is cold and damp. The weather seeps in. Papa was annoyed with the caretaker as he thinks the house has been neglected. For the first time, I heard one of his staff answer back, when the caretaker muttered something about there being a war on. I haven't seen Mark in three years, and not too much of Gerald either. I would have gone too, if someone had let me. They say it's awful, father tells me stories. He tells me about the politics of it too and how Kitchener was particularly infuriating. Kitchener was later killed when his ship hit a German mine on its way to Russia. Lloyd George had planned to go with him, but was prevented by problems in Ireland.

He and my father never did like the type of men who guard the old ways as if they are better. Papa made his fortune as a pioneer and I'm proud of him, but he's aged so much since the Food Ministry job and it has upset me to see him hounded by the press. At least he still has his work at the Port of London, though he's showing the first signs of becoming an old man.

I lie on my bed looking out, mesmerised by the swirling shapes of the mist. I keep imagining that Owen might walk out like an actor from behind a curtain. What would I do then? It is three years since I last saw him, but up here on the moor, the memory of him is alive. If he were to appear now, I would surely look at him for as long as I could without being seen. Of course, he would know if I was here.

As I watch the shifting cloud outside, I cannot help but remember another day like this, when we came for a short break in the spring of 1914. We were still naïve enough then, to think there would be no war.

*

We arrived on a fine day, and my heart delighted to see the house, prominent and majestic on its summit, as we drove up the green cutting. We had arrived early enough to see sunshine on the front façade, and the windows glinted like many eyes and I fancied that the house smiled to see us again. As we drew near, the breeze blew my hat off, so that I had to jump out of the car to collect it. Papa drove off, laughing and waving with Mama and the boys, leaving me behind. As I shrieked and ran after them, hopelessly out of breath, I saw a figure on the skyline, close to the house. Even though I could not see him clearly, I knew it was Owen. I only glanced at him, because my family were watching, but he was at the peat stack, collecting fuel. My heart fluttered and I slowed to a walk. When my family were far enough ahead, I replaced my hat and watched him at leisure. I was suddenly quite overpowered with my feelings for him, as if returning to Gwylfa had switched something on, and I was also rather confused as at that time I had just recently met Jonathan, and begun to set my sights on

145

him. Maybe I should have turned away from the sight of Owen, and not indulged myself in that way, but I enjoyed seeing him working. He was so quiet and handsome; there was something about his calm and methodical way of doing things, he was undistracted, with a certain grace.

He must have felt my eyes upon him, because he turned and looked. Stopped for a moment, still quite far off, and paused as if he was trying to see who approached. I checked that my family weren't watching—they were busy climbing out of the car—and I waved to him. I think he recognised me, because he turned back to his work with a new urgency. My heart sank, but I hoped that he was merely being discreet.

After I had eaten luncheon, I told my family I wanted to take a walk and much to my dismay, Mark joined me with his easel, so I couldn't look for Owen as I had hoped. Instead, we went out onto the moor and I followed my brother along a green-lipped path through the heather while he looked for a suitable viewpoint. As he walked before me, I admired him. He had finally grown taller, and broader of shoulder, though I was pleased he had retained his slim shape. It was becoming hard to decide who was more handsome out of Gerald and him.

'I'd like to paint you, sister,' he said, turning around to bestow a rare smile on me.

'Oh no, I would not keep still enough for you,' I replied. 'I'm too excited today.'

'Why are you so giddy?'

'I'm excited to be here again.'

'The heather is rather brown at this time of year and I need some colour. You could be the focal point.'

'No Mark, because you would want me for hours and I want to run about and explore. My dress is a brownish colour anyway, so I will not give you much colour.'

'You could change.'

'Maybe another day.'

I was so exuberant that Mark began to look suspicious and though he continued to cajole me, I knew I did not have the patience to sit for a painting when Owen might be near at hand. I had not forgotten our meetings in the summer of 1913. Mark persisted though, so I allowed him to make a few sketches of me as we sat in the heather.

'I'll have to remember this and see if I can capture the colours,' said Mark. 'You're glowing, Beryl and I like the way little wisps of your hair are escaping and blowing in the breeze.'

I laughed. I was delirious with anticipation and he could see it. The golden light of a late spring afternoon was all about us, my fawn dress matched the colour of the heather I was crushing as I sat, and all about us was birdsong, butterflies and bees.

'You're in love aren't you?' said Mark. 'Is it Jonathan?'

'I'm in love with life,' I replied and threw myself back into the heather to avoid his scrutiny; I could feel a blush rising to my cheeks.

'You can't fool me,' he said, looking down at me with a knowing look.

'And what ladies have you found in Oxford?' I asked. 'You never tell us of anything that happens there.'

'You never show any interest.'

*

That night, my maid, dear faithful Dora, took a note to Owen and reported to me that he took it with a serious look on his face, but she saw him smiling later, and much more exuberant than usual. Owen was not one for showing much excitement. I lay awake, my hope returned with a fervour and was restless in my bed, until an exhausted sleep took me.

The following day was not what I had hoped. Fog smothered the moor and the hour spent sitting on dry heather in the sun with Mark, was like a distant memory. Now it was all dampness and the ambience of the graveyard. As Dora helped me dress, I realised that the weather was ideal for my plan; it would make it easier to hide from scrutiny.

I was too nervous for eating, but I sat with my family obediently and ate as much as I could in order to not raise suspicion. Mark watched me, and asked again about a painting, but everyone else was engrossed in the food.

'It is supposed to clear later,' Papa said, motioning to the blanked out windows. 'We always get low cloud in the morning.'

After breakfast, I feigned a headache. The family retired to the drawing room, where a good fire was lit, but I put on a shawl and left the house through the terrace door on the south side; that way they would not see me.

I need not have worried, after a few steps away from the house I was lost in the fog, and as I looked back, some misgiving moved me. Owen might not come. I had never received any written answer from him, though I knew he could read and write. I would have to wait, and hope that he would understand my description of the meeting place. I had chosen a place that offered some shelter and a chance of being hidden. It was one of the semi-circular shooting butts, on a line running to the north of Gwylfa, close to the house, but far enough to be out of sight even on a clear day.

I had not gone much further and the house was already vanishing; little more than a large, grey silhouette behind me. Drawing my shawl around me, I continued until the low cloud stole the house away and I was alone, the fog spinning around me. I stopped and stood still, listening. There was no sound, save for a curlew cry from somewhere far to the north. A mixture of apprehension and excitement made me scattered of mind as I continued. It was some minutes before I realised that I had wandered off the sheep path that marked my route. I breathed deep of the damp, wet air and shuddered. I would have to try and retrace my steps and find the path. It was too risky to walk the moor without the known route, traps such as bogs awaited the foolhardy. I had left the house to the south but had then turned to trace a northerly route, but as I tried to track back, I found there was no landmark to guide my direction. It was then I realised how much a person relies on vision to create a mental compass.

I had put on a pale yellow dress, with a low sash and gossamer sleeves, but now regretted it. The dress was suited to summery days and already the thin material was beginning to feel damp and cold against me. It was hard walking through the heather too, it caught at the base of my dress and was crunchy and uncomfortable to step on. I was resigned by then to damaged shoes and dress, but still sought the path. Deep breaths were helping to calm me and I wondered whether to call for Owen. I decided not to, just in case the wrong person should hear.

I was relieved to come upon a sheep path, though not entirely sure if it were the same one. These paths allow an easy passage through the heather, and go nowhere in particular, except to follow convenient ways for sheep seeking pasture. I wondered if sheep ever sought adventure in the art of creating pathways, as this particular route took me mostly downward, occasionally rising and turning from earth to glinting rock. I hoped at least that it would not land me in a bog. I continued in what I hoped was the desired northerly direction. If the path was correct, I would reach the shooting butt within a few minutes. I tried to keep a sense of where I was going by looking around regularly, but with the grasping fog all around, was hopelessly disorientated. As I rearranged my shawl in attempt to cover the thin sleeves, I happened to feel my own flesh, and it was already as cold as that of a corpse.

The thought occurred to me that Owen might be blessed with more sense, and on seeing the dismal conditions, would not think to venture out. I was sure that by now, I should have reached the shooting butt, yet did not stop, it seemed more sensible to keep warm by moving. I decided to continue for a few more minutes and then to think about giving up. I was already beginning to admonish myself for such thoughtless and immoral behaviour, when I thought I saw a figure up ahead. Just a shape, standing still and obscured by the low cloud, a man's shape. I halted and looked ahead, guessing that if I could see him, then he could see me.

'Owen, is that you?'

The figure did not reply. Owen was a man of few words, so I moved onward.

'Owen, answer me, you are scaring me,' I said, hating to admit it and looking over my shoulder as goose bumps crawled the length of my arms.

When I looked ahead again, the figure was gone. It occurred to me then, that if it was Owen, this was an unkind trick to play. I stopped and looked about, thoroughly disorientated, my breaths coming shallow and a pulse pounding in my ears. It was time to return to the house. I turned around to walk back in the opposite direction, but stopped in my tracks when once again the figure appeared before me, indistinct in the churning fog. I wondered at how he had gotten around me without a sound and without the path? I decided there must be another path nearby, because I would have surely heard him stumbling through the heather.

'Speak, whoever you are,' I said, trying to sound confident and unperturbed; which was the opposite of how I felt. My mind was already busy deciding on who this phantom might be, and after I had ruled out Owen or another member of our staff, I could only think that it was a poacher or some other kind of ruffian, that did not want to announce himself. I had already realised that I might be in danger, but had no weapon about my person and was resigned to trying to talk my way out of it.

'If you are trespassing, you had best be on your way,' I said loudly, 'I will not report you or get in your way.'

Still, the figure did not reply, though it appeared to be turned towards me, and wearing some sort of oddly-shaped tall hat that I could not decipher the detail of.

'Papa, I'm coming back now,' I shouted, as a sudden panic gripped me. Let this creature think there was another man close by and maybe it would scarper.

I folded my arms to protect myself and began walking in earnest towards it, but as soon as I was walking, I noted that it appeared further away. There, I thought, that moved him on.

Yet I was not being entirely honest with myself, for the movement of this effigy was not altogether normal. No living person can move without some sort of rocking in their gait. This thing was moving away from me, but smoothly, as if it could glide, and it still appeared to be turned towards me. How can a person move backwards smoothly like that? I did not care to answer my own question. My breathing was ragged as I walked, pushing myself onward, determined to retain an appearance of calm. Perhaps my senses were playing tricks. All I had to do was close my eyes and reopen them, and it would be gone. So I slowed my pace and tore my gaze away from the thing, screwed my eyes shut and whispered prayers.

'Please, please, please, go!' When I opened my eyes, there was nothing ahead of me but the fog. It was oddly like being in a capsule, despite the fact that I was on open moor, the thick grey cloud about me was walling me in. I increased my pace, now that I was alone again. The strange figure must have been my own imagining, brought on by fear and overactive senses. I pushed onward, speaking calm words to myself in order to control the unearthly terror that had me in its grip.

It was then that I felt as if there were a presence behind me again, and I lamented that I was not alone after all. Something was coming up fast and close. I whirled around, my throat gripped by the hand of my own fear. Nothing. Yet out of the side of my eye, I thought something moved and when I stopped and turned to look, it was gone. Again it happened, as if something were running circles around me, but not allowing me to see it, always in the side vision and then, gone. I knew that I was close to real panic and that I would bolt and run headlong, if I let that panic take hold. I stopped to breathe and tried to calm myself, there was no sense in trying to outrun anything dressed as I was. I must catch my breath first and calm myself. But it was no use, standing still was not helping either, my breath was coming in strange, short wheezes, and I was gasping like fish drowning on a deck.

I was about to press on, when I heard a strange metallic sound from behind; a clanking noise. As I turned, I came eye to eye with a face that was dark-eyed and fierce, partly clothed in metal with helmet and headdress. I screamed an oddly weak sound that strangled in my throat and turned to run in panic, my breathing coming in awful rasps, and my back prickling and cold in my terror. I tripped and fell to the floor, crying in fear that I would now be caught by this creature, whatever it might be, but looked up only to see the fog crowding around me. I must have looked a miserable wretch as I crawled, crying in fear between gulps of air. Realising the absurdity of my position, I picked myself up, lifted my skirts, and ran. My wits were no longer with me, I only knew to run as fast as my restrictive attire allowed, and so it was that I did not see a figure loom up before me until too late and ran right into it. I screamed at it and hit out, finding that my fists connected with a soft, woollen coat and when I looked up I saw Owen's face looking down at me in surprise and shock. What I looked like to him, I can only guess. My words tumbled out of me, as I tried to tell him there was a strange man on the moor. Owen hugged me to him and I felt the thundering in his chest, almost enough to match mine.

'Be still,' he said quietly, 'you are safe with me.'

There was something oddly calming about his presence that had an immediate effect on me, and I put my arms around his waist with tears of relief, and saw my own fickleness as my mind filled with a lightheaded love for him, and fear was banished away.

'Owen, I thought you weren't coming.'

'I did consider not coming,' said Owen's voice from above me, and I lifted my face to look at him. 'But then I guessed that my wild lady would be alone in the fog, and I could not leave her.'

'Why were you not going to come?'

'You know it is no use, Beryl.'

'I think it is. You have saved me. I might have died of fright, but now I am quite cured of it, here in your arms.'

Still, I strained my neck around to look behind and check the thing was really gone.

'I can't see anything,' said Owen as he pulled me tighter to him and I felt his lips press against the top of my head.

'Let's get you back,' he said quietly. 'You're shaking.'

'I am cold,' I admitted, 'and I was very frightened only a minute ago. Those are two good reasons to shake, but I'm shaking for a different reason now.'

I looked into his eyes, and thought then that they were like the colour of pale spring skies over Hiraethog, and I noticed that he was shaking too.

'Don't take me back yet,' I said. 'It will make me sad, if I only get this little time with you. I will be warm enough with you holding me. We have so little time together, let us make it worthwhile so that we have something to live on when we're apart.'

'Come then,' he said, placing his arm around my shoulder, 'we will go to your chosen meeting place.'

'Are we near?'

'Yes,' he said as he pulled me off the path and within several paces, we had found the section of horseshoe-shaped stone wall and turf that served as shelter and camouflage for shooters.

Owen laid out his coat and rejected my attempt to offer the shawl.

'You need to keep warm,' he said. 'My clothes are warmer than yours.'

We sat down in the limited shelter given by the low wall and the marsh grass that grew tall over it, and I leaned against him.

'Why do you think it is no use?' I asked.

'You know why,' he said softly. 'You are of a different class, no good can come of us.'

'I am not truly of that class you are thinking of,' I said. 'My father is an ordinary man, he earned his title through his talent for business and politics. There was no Lord Devonport before him.'

He smiled down at me, though his eyes were sad. 'It matters not. He will not want his only daughter with a servant.'

'Is what I want not important?' I asked, grasping his hand in mine. 'I have been pursuing you for years, Owen, why should I change my mind now? It was you that ran from me, for so long.'

He laughed. 'I thought it was all some game of yours. Rich folk often use the poor as amusements.'

'Not me,' I said, indignantly. 'It's just the same as it was last year; you're all I see.'

'I admit I have thought of you often in the months since our last meeting. I tried not to, but couldn't help myself.'

'Do you love me as I love you?' I asked him.

He looked sideways at me, and I caught my breath. His dark hair contrasted dramatically with his pale skin. I touched his cheekbone and ran my finger along it, embarrassed at what I'd admitted to.

I waited for a reply but it didn't come. I was not too much perturbed, for I had always believed in Owen. This relationship was nothing ordinary. I was determined to do my best to win him over.

'There must be a way we can be together,' I said. 'Let me think on it.'

'Your mind will be changed in the end; they will find you a match.'

'Do not talk like that.'

'Have they not already found someone for you?'

'Let us not speak of it,' I said, taking his face in my hands. 'I love you, Owen.'

I saw the doubt cross his face, he knew as well as I that I had avoided answering him.

'And now please kiss me,' I moved towards him until his lips found mine. I sensed some reluctance on his part at first, for though his lips brushed mine, he was tense. I didn't want to lose him, so I kissed him with all the passion I felt, and a light energy thrilled through me. There are no words that can do justice to that kind of heady first love, and the dizzy high it brings. Perhaps we looked clumsy from the outside as our faces drew close and our lips met. I do not know, but I think the power of all that feeling in me reached him too, because he suddenly returned my kisses with a passion and gripped me tight against him.

I no longer knew where I was, beyond the feel of his arms, his mouth, his body. I opened my eyes and found him looking at me, and was ecstatic, my happiness and love for this person was close to unbearable, I could hardly breathe. Did the fear of the figure in the mist, heighten my senses? I know not, but I have not felt the like of it since.

We had rehearsed for this before, in our brief meetings. Once we were unclothed, our bodies pressed together in a unity that I swoon at the mere remembrance of. We held one another like fanatics; ardent, yet tender, and unaware of the cold fog that clawed at us and the damp that seeped through his coat and my shawl. We only became aware of that later, when we tried to hold one another, but had to help each other dress as our flesh grew cold.

We sat for a while, wrapped up together, surprised at ourselves and ignoring the discomfort of damp heather. We made the most of each other's warmth and the shelter from the biting breezes that whipped the grasses. The fog was no longer so heavy and I remembered that father had said it would lift.

'Well, there is no going back now,' I said, when we had been quiet for a while.

'You should not shame yourself with me,' said Owen.

I put my finger on his lips to quiet him. 'You must not say that,' I scolded. 'Don't spoil it with mere words.'

'You are surprising, Beryl. I never knew someone so determined to be free,' he said, after he'd removed my finger from his lips and kissed it.

'I am determined to be treated fairly,' I said. 'When I was young, I thought myself equal to my brothers. Later, I learned different, but that hasn't stopped me wanting to be like them. I don't think that Gerald will settle for many years yet.'

'The maids think him handsome.'

'Tell the maids to steer clear.'

'That would be hypocritical of me,' he said, with a smile.

I laughed at that.

'I admire the spirit in you,' he said. 'You inspire me to think with more ambition for myself.'

'Do I? Oh I'm so glad to hear that,' I said and I kissed his cold cheek quite fiercely. 'If we are both prepared to fight, then maybe there will be some hope for us.'

I watched his face as I said this, and saw the rueful look. 'My dear,' I said. 'Don't doubt it. My family are only here for a short break, but we will be back in a few months for the summer. Mama and I have some charity events, but I will work on her and see if she will not let me come up earlier. I will tell her that I need a rest, and fresh air.'

'When will you come?'

'July, I hope, but in August we will definitely be here. In the meantime, I will plan our approach. At some point I will have to confront my parents and we will both have to be very strong for a while. They will try to break us apart, but we must not be cowed. You must be steadfast, and don't let your parents or mine break your resolve. I just wish it were easier for us to communicate.'

'Dora is a good friend,' said Owen, tightening his arm around me.

'Yes,' I agreed. 'I can get her to post a letter to you, telling you when I'm coming. I will get her to sign it in her own hand. That will save you from suspicion, should anyone chance to read it. But remember, the letter will be from me, my love, and not Dora.'

Owen laughed, and then looked at me in that endearingly shy manner. He held his hand over his chest. 'I can wait, if you promise to return to me.'

I was overjoyed at this admission from him. It was the most he had ever given.

'Of course I will, I promise you here and now,' I said, laying my hand over his. My eyes pricked with tears at the corners. 'I love you, my dear,' I said and I waited, with tears crowding in for his answer.

Owen bowed his head and smiled, looked at my hand over his and whispered back to me: 'I love you too, Beryl.'

We kissed as if to seal our word and when he finally pulled away from me, he spoke with a new strength.

'I'm not afraid of what they'll say. With you by my side, I feel like I can do anything,' he said, and I looked in wonder at the confidence that had arisen in him.

'Your words are like nectar to me,' I said, hugging him tightly. 'Let me look at you, I have to remember you.'

Owen was solemn, but with the slightest of smiles he returned my gaze. Our eyes locked and I tried my best to hold myself steady as I was now the shy one. I felt myself blush, but I did not want to give up on looking at him. We found each other's hands and I felt the heat of him. My breaths came fast, and I made myself take a deep, steadying one and breathed him into my heart. I wanted to cry, but we both laughed when we could hold on no longer. I don't think he saw the two tears that fell, and if he did, I hope he knew they were tears of happiness.

'What did you see earlier?' Owen asked, after we had fallen quiet again.

'I don't know exactly,' I said. 'I was terrified, until I found you and now I am ecstatically happy. It matters not.'

'People do sometimes see things on the moors,' he said, looking thoughtfully out into the fog. 'Look, it's clearing.'

It was indeed lifting and the view around us had expanded.

'It was just a strange, blurred thing,' I said. 'I thought it was you at first, but it did not answer when I spoke. Even then I thought it was you, for you do not always answer me.'

Owen smiled at that.

'It was too much hidden, to be clearly seen, but then for an instant, it was right in front of my face, too close to see clearly, but I saw dark eyes staring at me and metal over part of the face, like a helmet.'

'A helmet,' said Owen. 'Oh. Was it a Roman centurion?'

'Yes, I think it was. It just flashed in front of my eyes, then I screamed and it was gone, but I did see the helmet around its face and a plume above. I suppose you think me mad—'

'No, Beryl. I don't because it has been seen before in these parts.'

'Oh, I have not heard of it.'

'Yes, they say it is a ghost that lingers, it has been seen at the stone bridge and folk say it guards the bridge as perhaps it did in life. But it has been seen on the moor too.'

'Goodness, so that is what I saw,' I hugged Owen tighter, as I thought of this and wondered why he looked so sad. 'What is it? Is there more to tell?'

'Oh it's nothing,' he said.

'You can't say that, my mind will create all kinds of horrific tales. You must tell me if there is more, if only to save me from myself.'

'It's just stories,' he said. 'I'm sure my mother just wanted to stop me wandering about.'

'Hurry and tell me dear.'

He gripped my hand and looked at me: 'They say that if you see the Roman centurion, that it's an omen of death.'

21

I could see by his face that he invested too much belief in these local tales, but I refused to. I swallowed the tightness in my throat and said: 'I don't believe in that sort of thing. You are quite right in thinking that folk tell these stories to frighten their children.'

'Even if it is true,' he said, still looking a trifle too serious for my liking, 'then it doesn't mean that *you* will die. It might be someone else. Someone you know.'

He looked down and shook his head then, and I realised he was admonishing himself for saying too much.

'I'm not worried,' I said, squeezing his arm. 'Because I don't believe in it.'

'Even so,' he removed his arm from my shoulders and took both of my hands in his, 'I would like to take the curse from you, because I'd rather it was me than you.'

'Oh I do love you,' I said, laughing, though I was deeply moved. 'There is no curse and you must not give it power by talking as if it were true. I do not want you to die either, let us not talk anymore of this.'

I kissed him hard on the lips, to show him my love and my certainty that I was right. I could see that he was an innocent, who had seen less of the modern world and its ways than I. As I kissed him I was determined that he would see much more, with me by his side.

'Before we go, can I ask you for something?' I said.

'Yes, anything,' he spoke softly and with a sincerity, that melted me away to nothing.

'I would like a lock of your hair, Owen. Something to remember you by. Can you get that to me? I will give you a photograph of me if you want it. Dora will bring it, and will you send a bit of hair back to me in return?'

'Of course,' he said. 'As I have no photographs of me to give.'

'That is a shame,' I said. 'For one as beautiful as you should be painted and photographed hundreds of times.'

Owen blushed at that.

'We had better go back separately,' I said. 'People may be missing us, we are out visiting tomorrow, but the day after I can try—'

I was stopped by the sound of someone approaching, the unmistakeable rustling of marsh grass. Owen and I stared at each other wide-eyed, and I put my finger to my lips to ask for his silence, and then stood to face whoever it was. With the improving visibility, I could see a man approaching, at first I feared it was Papa, but this figure was too tall and slim.

'Mark,' I said. 'What are you doing here?'

'I could ask you the same,' he grunted as he slipped on the damp grass.

I realised I must act fast if I was to conceal Owen and explain my dishevelled appearance.

'Oh Mark, am I glad to see you.' I climbed the bank and tried to dissuade him from coming closer. 'I was so afraid.'

'Why is your hair all down like that?' asked Mark, eyeing me suspiciously.

'It came undone,' I said stepping towards him. 'I saw a ghost, and I ran in terror from it.'

Mark smiled as if he doubted me.

'It is true. I can swear it is. I saw a Roman centurion, and I am not the only person to have seen this spectre. Have you not heard the story of it?' I gripped his arm, but Mark shook his head.

'Beryl, dear sister, I do not believe you.'

'Why not?'

'Because you are not running now are you? In fact I heard voices and so I came towards the sound. Mama had discovered that you were not in the house and was frightfully worried. So here I am, sent to find you.'

'I was talking to myself,' I said, drawing my shawl around me and attempting to tidy my hair from my face. 'I'm ready to go back now, I thank you for finding me.'

Mark ignored me and began to move past me, towards the shooting butt. I tried to stop him with my hand, but he pushed it away and continued, I wanted to shout a warning to Owen but knew it was too late. In a last attempt to stop him, I pulled on Mark's coat, but he had already seen Owen.

There was anger in my brother's eyes when he turned to look back at me.

'I knew it!' he said, with a vicious pleasure that I did not like.

Owen had stood up and was now in view. He held his cap in his hands, but I was pleased, in spite of everything to see a look of defiance on his face.

'You have ruined yourself, sister! What were you thinking?' Mark looked me up and down in disgust and I became aware that my dress was torn and dirty.

'The only thing that is ruined is my dress,' I said boldly, raising my chin. 'And I refuse to be spoken to like this by my youngest brother. This man is my friend, that is all.'

Mark laughed nastily, and inside I was shocked that he could be so malicious.

'You do not fool me for a minute, Beryl. I have seen it in your eyes and your manner.'

'He is just my friend and you have nothing on me. He rescued me after I saw the ghost and I was thanking him.'

'How exactly did you go about thanking him?'

'I will not answer that,' I said, ignoring the innuendo. 'I was quite lost and if Owen had not found me, who knows, I still would be lost. Maybe I would be drowned in a bog. Maybe you would prefer that.'

Mark turned to Owen and I stepped towards the two, trying to get between them before anything happened to make things worse. I looked at Owen, hoping that he would not try to fight with Mark, but found that he was looking at me, with an odd look that I did not understand until later.

'Wait until I tell my father,' said Mark, looking at Owen, his fists closed and knuckles white. 'You will be dismissed for this.'

'Go back to the house,' I told Owen, 'I will sort this out.'

'Yes, go back and pack your bags,' said Mark.

Owen glanced one last time at me, and then left us. I was sorry to see his face like that, upset and close to tears. Now it was my turn to be angry.

'Why did you have to be so nasty? Frightening him like that. He has done nothing wrong!'

'I don't believe you. I thought it was strange that you were so happy. At first I guessed it was the meeting with Jonathan at the party last month, but that did not quite fit. You had only met once and danced once, and you had not appeared any different than usual until we came here.'

Mark was right and there was little I could do to outmanoeuvre him, except to continue my denial.

'I like Owen. He is my friend and he came here at my request. We talked that is all.'

Mark smiled and looked me up and down again.

'Who knows what I might have seen if I had arrived at this place ten minutes earlier,' he said.

'How dare you!' I cried, and I slapped him for his insolence.

He put a hand to his reddened cheek and fixed me with a furious stare. 'Father will hear of this,' he said. 'Now come back to the house with me.'

He did not stop to see if I would follow but walked ahead purposefully. I ran after him, ready to beg.

'I apologise for hitting you,' I said. 'Your accusations made me angry. You must not tell Papa, please!'

He was walking at a vigorous pace and I had to run to keep up.

'Please Mark, I beg you. Owen is my friend. He must not suffer for my sins!'

Mark stopped and grabbed hold of my wrist. 'Admit the truth and I might consider.'

'You will only consider. That is not enough.'

Mark hesitated. 'If you tell me the truth, and you pose for the painting I want, then I will not tell father, *this* time.'

I took a breath in and let it out slowly as I thought this over. His eyes were intent on me as he relaxed his hold on my wrist and let me go.

'I will do the portrait.'

'This afternoon,' said Mark. 'Wear your violet dress.'

'If I do, you must not tell,' I said.

'Violet will suggest the flowering of the heather at a time when it isn't. Rather clever don't you think?'

I realised that my brother cared so much for art, that it was the only way to bargain with him.

'Yes Mark. You are a good brother. Can I rely on you to keep this quiet?'

'Was I right?' asked Mark. I could see that his expression had softened and this gave me hope.

'Yes,' I sighed. 'It was all me. I pursued him. Please whatever you do, or whatever you think, remember that. I want to protect him.'

'Do you love him?'

I nodded. 'With every cell of my living body.'

Mark surprised me then by hugging me and I, being in the high emotional state that I was that day, cried into his jacket. He held me while I sobbed, finally releasing me and taking my hand.

'I will tell them I found you. The ghost story will explain the state of you, if they see you, but I think it best if you steal in through the terrace way if you can. They're taking tea in the library so don't walk that way.'

'Thank you dearest brother,' I said, squeezing his hand.

'You have to stop seeing him Beryl.'

I did not reply to that.

*

Afterward, when I had time to think it over, and I relived it so many times, I realised why Owen had looked oddly at me. It had been a look of disappointment. He had been ready then to stand and face Mark as my lover, and I had denied him. I had thought myself the stronger one, but in truth he had stood up and been prepared to lose everything. I cannot excuse myself, except to say that I had wanted time to formulate a plan, to think of how to do it. In reality, I know that there could be no real plan, we just needed to be strong, or else spend our lives snatching brief liaisons in forsaken places.

I suspect that Mark may have sent some warning my father's way. I cannot be sure. We made no real promise on it, but I stood patiently for his painting in the violet dress as he requested. I was not pleased when I saw the finished painting.

Mark had painted me wonderfully, standing proudly on the moor, looking more beautiful than I could ever hope to be, but there was a figure in the background. He claimed that he had painted the ghost in, on a whim, but to me the figure looked more like the silhouette of Owen than a Roman centurion. Either way, I was not pleased.

No one took my ghost story too seriously and as time has gone on, I too wonder if it was just an apparition of my overwrought senses.

I gave Owen my photograph through Dora, and he sent me the lock of hair, and that was the last I heard of him. I wrote to him, through Dora, as we had agreed, but then the war came, so we did not visit Gwylfa as planned in the summer of 1914. I later heard from Mark, that Owen had enlisted and I took to bed early on that particular night, and spent it in sorrow. He had never written to me. What did that mean? I wrote him another letter, professing my undying love, and asked that he return to me when he could, telling him that I would be ready to tell the world of our love.

As the war progressed, class distinction seemed a trifling thing compared to the horrors that were happening at home and abroad, and everywhere I looked, people were throwing the old conventions to the wind. My letter became tear-stained as I read it again and again, adding more, until it filled several pages, but I did not know where to send it. By then our staff had reduced and Dora had moved on. Mark was uncooperative and so I burnt it.

All the while, my family and the Parkers were nudging me towards Jonathan. He was a kind man, who began to win a part of my heart. He could never win it all, as Owen had.

I resisted for a time, by remembering Owen. It was easy to relive that last day on the moor at first, but as time went on, the part of the memory with Mark, and the look of disappointment on Owen's face began to intrude on the happy memory, and I began to doubt. I wondered if I had lost Owen back there on the moor, when I failed to stand up in front of him and admit the truth to my brother. Of course I did admit the truth to Mark after, but Owen did not know of that, and I had not thought to include it in the letter I sent. I wished for the chance to go back and change that mistake.

In 1916, while he was on leave, with minor injuries, Jonathan proposed to me and I recklessly accepted. Afterward, I doubted whether I had done the right thing and wanted to retract it, but the happiness in Jonathan's eyes and the celebrations of our two families stayed my hand. It was more than two years since I had seen Owen by then, and my hope had faded. I had seen London bombed and the Grim Reaper had visited every town, if not every street in the country. I tried to push Mark to find out any news of Owen, even just to tell me if he was alive, but Mark was more than reluctant to indulge me and was encouraging me to acknowledge Jonathan.

I try to imagine what I would do if Owen were to appear now, out there in the mist as he is in Mark's painting. The decent part of me would want to avoid him and ignore him, to pretend it all never happened. After all, I am now engaged. However, the decent part of me is but a small part, and I know that I would run to him and throw myself into his arms, and having lost him once, would not allow it to happen again.

Would Jonathan still marry me if he knew? Maybe if I confessed to him, he would break the engagement off for me.

It does not seem right that I lie on a soft bed, while my two men are at war, maybe already dead. I would like to be working more for the war effort, it would keep my mind occupied, but apart from Mama permitting me to act as nurse to a few officers, I have not been allowed much. I'm happy to hear that Lloyd George has achieved equal pay for the women who are working alongside the men in the war effort and hopefully votes will come soon. If I marry Jonathan, I will be more in charge of my life then. I think he would allow me that and I have always avoided men who appear domineering. Yet still, I cannot help but wish for Owen.

With a sudden thought, I jump off my bed and make for the door. It has lately been my fate to wait, but I am a woman of action, and now my feet carry me quietly down the stairs towards the corridor that connects to the servant's quarters. With few staff now in our employ, this area of the house is mostly empty. I hesitate at the arched wooden door, and check that I am not observed before going through. I have a fancy to find the room that Owen used when he was here. He was one of our local workers, and only stayed when we were up for a visit. I realise that I know nothing about his life outside of this house, and regret that I did not learn more in our limited time.

Before I recruited Dora to relay messages, I often wandered into this part of the house. The original wooden house, Plas Pren, was built when I was ten years old, and in the early days I'd go to the kitchens to watch Mrs Findlay, our Scottish cook. On a few occasions she let me help with some minor food preparation, but mostly she gave me a cake and shooed me away.

I first spotted Owen when I was seventeen, and was immediately struck by him. I took to finding reasons to go into the servant's quarters, whenever I could in the hope of seeing him, but he was elusive. I often got up early, so that I could catch him making the fires and that was how I managed to start up conversations with him. It worked well, for a while, and I had managed to make him laugh a few times, which delighted me, but then Papa found out and I was banned from talking to him. I was so drawn to him, that I might have ignored the prohibition sooner, but for Papa's threat to dismiss him if I was caught talking to him again.

It is many years since I entered this part of the house. It looks shabbier than I remember and all the doors are closed. The men's rooms are on the downstairs corridor and the women's are above. His room was the middle one. As far I know, no one else has used it since he left. Looking around, to check no one sees me, I try the handle and am happy to find it open. I slip inside and close it softly behind me.

It is a small room, with a simple wooden desk, a stool, a wardrobe, chest of drawers and a bed. It looks like he has taken most of his belongings away, but as I turn round I see an old coat hanging on the back of the door and I recognise it as the one he wore that day on the moor. I run my hand over it and bring it to my nose, inhaling. There is the acrid odour of old peat smoke ingrained in the fabric, but I inhale harder to see if I can detect a smell of him. I end up sneezing loudly and then stand frozen, afraid that I will have alerted someone to my intrusion. There is no sound and no one comes. I take the coat down and put it on over my dress, hugging it to me. Then I lie down on his mattress, wondering if he lay here, thinking of me. I close my eyes and pretend he is here now, next to me. Everything here smells of peat smoke, but if I think back, that is what Owen smelled of.

I came in hope of finding something left for me, and though this hope is slim, I get up and begin opening the drawers and the wardrobe, and even feel the underside of his desk. The sense that I am intruding, is overcome by a desperate wish to find some token. I even look for cracks in the joints of his furniture where a missive could be lodged.

After I have looked through what furniture there is, I peruse the room, begging it to give up its secrets. The cracks around his window catch my eye and I see something lodged there. I cannot get hold of it with my fingers, but a hairpin does the trick. I know what it is as soon as I see it. The picture I gave him to remember me by. Why has he left it?

The sound of a door closing nearby alerts me that I'm no longer alone. The maid is back, and I must leave for fear of being seen. I push the photo back into the crack, replace the coat, and slip out.

I have no more answers than before, and will have to be patient. I hurry back along the corridor and into the hallway. No one has seen me and I head for the main staircase.

The house is oddly quiet; I hear the murmur of voices from the library and guess it is Papa talking to the vicar and Ralph. I drift upstairs towards my room, thinking that I might take a nap, when there is a sudden loud knocking, coming from the front door. Turning round, I head back downstairs, into the hallway where I feel damp air and cool breezes as the door is opened. The maid has answered it, but Mama is there too.

'Telegram, ma'am,' says a voice, and I see a young man in uniform at the door. My breathing has become rapid. Mama is just staring at the envelope and the telegram boy is already leaving.

'What is it?' I ask.

Mama has opened it quickly and impatiently, tearing it with shaking hands and reading it in the most agitated way that I have ever seen her read anything.

'Mama?'

She gives a little cry, and the hand that holds the telegram drops to her side while the other claps to her mouth. She turns to me.

'Tell me!' I cry—it is unbearable not knowing. But will it be more unbearable when I do know?

'It's from the Parker family,' she says, and looks at me. Her eyes are wide and then she closes them and drops the telegram.

From the Parker's? My mind races as Mama sobs and a maid helps her back into the main part of the house. I retrieve the telegram and Papa is at my side before I have finished reading. There are not many words to read and it's not even grammatically correct, though I wonder why I should care about that now.

'Jonathan's dead,' is all I can manage to say.

Papa takes me in his arms and holds me up as my knees try to give way.

'Oh, I am sorry,' he says.

I'm aware of Ralph and the vicar further down the hallway. They appear as shadowy figures in the gloom and are distant.

'I can't believe it,' I say. I feel numb at first, but then something else creeps in. I suppose it is guilt.

'Don't be afraid, cry as much as you have to,' says Papa. 'I had heard that the campaign at Messines had been a success for the British and hoped for better news than this. It is a dark day that this should happen to you my dear child.'

22

The day before we left Hiraethog, to return to Wittington, Owen's father came to see Papa. After he had driven away, Papa came out of the library looking ashen-faced.

'What's wrong?' I asked him.

He looked at me in a distracted way and then appeared to see me properly. His mouth opened and then closed. 'Don't worry Beryl,' he said. 'I just need to see your Mother.'

'She's in the drawing room,' I said.

Something made me follow him. He did not see me and once I knew that no one was around, I put my ear to the door. I am not one for eavesdropping, but on this occasion perhaps it was a mercy that my father did not tell me to my face. I was still shaken by Jonathan's death, and not ready to hear worse.

I heard my father tell Mama that he had bad news for her. I was already bracing myself as I leaned against the door, yet it still felt as if someone had run me through with a bayonet when I heard the words: 'Owen is dead. He died at the battle of Messines...'

They may have heard the door rattle as I pulled away from it in an anguish of horror. I was cold all over, it was a feeling that I never would want to repeat. My last hopes for the future were extinguished.

I bolted like a rabid animal, out of the house and onto the moor. I ran until Gwylfa grew small and I was breathless and wheezing. Then I screamed his name into the sky. My gasping state did not allow me to scream loudly, but I did so repeatedly until my throat was sore and then threw myself down into the heather and sobbed for what felt like an age. If there was any doubt as to whom I'd loved more, this reaction removed it.

After that I wandered for a while, revisiting the places where Owen and I had met. When I reached the shooting butt, I watched the grass blown flat in the breeze and thought of how it looked different in the sun. I remembered that foggy day, with Owen very much alive. How could I still be here, without him?

I wiped my eyes and watched a butterfly flitting about the heather and felt the heat of the sun on my arms, while wondering how such a beautiful day could feel so terrible. Something made me think of the Roman centurion and I scanned the horizon in all directions, willing it to come and take me. But of course, a ghost never appears when you want it to.

If either of my parents wondered why my grief took a turn for the worse at that time, they did not say anything about it to me. Mark knew, and he sympathised. Maybe he was burdened by some guilt, because he found out all he could and relayed some of it to me, though I suspect some upsetting detail may have been held back.

I was told that Owen had acquitted himself with bravery. It pained me to think of that quiet and dignified person thrown into a world of horror, where he was expected to kill or be killed. There was no message for me, and Owen had never taken my picture with him, so no one knew of our connection. Part of me wanted to tell them all, to do what I should have done before, but I realised it would be selfish. It was his family's grief too, not just mine.

A month later, Owen's death brought Dora back to me. She wrote to me, telling me that she had something important to tell me and that it could not wait. I was to meet her in London where she was now working as a housekeeper. This revelation created a rising bubble of hope in my chest. I would find out something more about Owen, and some of my questions might be answered. I tried not to hope for too much, because nothing would change the fact that he was dead.

We met at a café in London, one miserable wet day in late July. It was the first time I'd felt alive in over a month. Dora shook my hand, rather formally and we ordered coffee. She was well-turned out in a belted tunic with a full skirt in a becoming shade of green that set off her flame red hair, and I was pleased that she had been promoted, though she promised me that it was nothing special.

'You look very well Dora.'

'Thank you,' she said, looking momentarily at me, before casting her eyes down. She was too honest to return the compliment and I knew well enough what I looked like. I had seen my pale face with the huge dark circles under my eyes. The black hat and coat I wore only served to drain my colour further. I looked like something undead.

'Congratulations on your promotion,' I said.

'It's not like it was before the war,' she replied, looking up. 'It is just a small staff.'

There was a look of apprehension in her eyes and I could wait no longer to hear her news.

'Tell me what you've come to say, I must hear it,' I said.

'Please forgive me, Beryl.'

'I don't know what you are talking about.'

'I meant to tell you before now,' she said, her nerves getting the better of her, as her voice cracked and she swallowed hard.

'What? Please just tell me.'

'I'm afraid you'll be angry.'

'I won't. But I must know.'

'Owen wrote you a letter before he left and he told me to retrieve it and give it to you.'

'Do you have it?' I asked eagerly, my hands gripping the table edge.

'No,' she shook her head and I saw that she was close to tears. 'It's hidden. At Gwylfa. I was supposed to get it when we next visited, but I changed job so of course I didn't go with you. I kept thinking that I must tell you, but I was so busy with the new place, and I kept putting it off. Oh, I'm so ashamed.'

'Don't be,' I said, placing my hand on hers. 'Just tell me, can I still see this letter?'

'Yes, well at least I think so. It's hidden in Owen's room at Gwylfa.'

I listened as Dora described the location.

'That's strange,' I said.

'What is?'

'I have looked there already. I found my photograph there, but no letter.'

'Oh.'

'Do you know what he said in it?' I asked.

Dora shook her head. 'It would have been before he left in the autumn of 1914.'

I bit my lip. 'Maybe it was there and I just didn't see it.'

'Yes,' said Dora hopefully. 'You must look again and let me know if you do find it.'

'Maybe it is the reply to my letter that I waited for.'

'I'm so sorry,' said Dora, tears beginning to stream down her cheeks. 'It's unforgiveable of me.'

'I wish you had told me earlier,' I said, 'but I forgive you. Please don't cry.'

'And I'm sorry that it didn't work out for you and Owen,' she said, taking out a handkerchief and blowing her nose rather unceremoniously.

'What do you mean by that?' I asked.

'Oh, just that you didn't get to be together,' said Dora. 'I so wanted you to be a couple.'

'I did too,' I said, and reached into my pocket for my own handkerchief.

*

At first I was desperate to get hold of the letter, and I asked repeatedly if we could visit Gwylfa, but my parents were adamant that we would not go again until the following summer, and there was no one I could ask at the house.

I even thought of going alone, but realised I couldn't do so without making them suspect my sanity. I suppose I was a frightful coward, but something happened to me over that year of grieving, and by the end of it I was not the same headstrong young woman. Exhausted by grief, I no longer wanted to see the letter.

Neither could I be too caught up in my own drama for death was all around and there was much that Mama and I could do to help the living. When I next stood within the walls of Gwylfa, it was 1918, and I knew that I was healing. To read the letter would have returned me to mourning. Owen had either decided he no longer wanted me, or had written me a letter of love. It was a moment in time, now passed. I concluded that to read the letter, would be to undo the healing that had begun. It was better not to know, though I was sorely tempted from time to time. Part of me was curious just to see what kind of writer he was.

I understood by then, that Owen and I had ended before we'd ever begun, and on quite an unnatural high. I lament that our last time was a day so charged and so overly romanticised in my memory. Nothing can reach that vertiginous height again. I never got to see him as the flawed human being that he really was.

I watched my friends fall in love, marry, bicker and grow bored and wondered what would have happened if Owen had survived. Something exceptional would have become ordinary over time. I longed to go back and change the past, so that we could have had that chance. I blamed the war, blamed Papa, Mark, myself. But maybe Owen would have died anyway, even without the war. Some people are marked that way.

If I could go back, I would take his hand and stand in front of my parents with him. I would tell them that I loved him. Then, whatever happened after, at least there would be no regret.

Mark mentioned the centurion a few times, but I refused to believe any of that.

'You lost two men,' he said.

'To the war,' I replied.

23

Gwen

March 1954

Mam and Tad have returned with Dewi and both were very emotional in different ways when they saw Alis. Mam was happy with lots of tears and Tad was angry, although he's not sure who to be angry at, Alis herself, or Dewi and me. He is lucky he didn't see the state of her. At least I saved him that. It seemed the right thing to do and I thought it would help get her on my side, but now, she's got a sly look about her and I'm beginning to think that I may as well have not bothered.

Mam has confiscated the black bracelet and the brooch, but I have the necklace still, hidden under my clothes.

We're sitting in conference around the kitchen table, Mam and Tad are at each end, with Dewi and me on one side and Alis on the other. We only ever sit like this for a meeting when something quite serious has happened and I suppose that this is the most serious thing ever.

'You can clean that moustache off your face as well when we've finished here,' Tad says sharply, looking at me as if I am an object of disgust. I find myself nodding meekly and then catch Alis smirking at me. She is plotting something, but I will do all I can to thwart her.

'What happened after you went into the house together?' asks Mam.

'Well,' Alis looks down at her finger which is drawing circles with the spilt milk on the table top. 'We went out into the hallway and started talking about the fireplace and Dewi was saying how I'm the right size to go up and clean the chimney. And then,' she stops stirring with her finger and takes a gulp of milk. I stare at her as she purposely draws it out. I try to stare in such a way that she might feel strobes of light coming out of my eyes and into her. Strobes that control her and make her say the right thing.

'Come on Alis,' says Tad impatiently. 'Just tell us.'

Mam gives Tad a look. 'Do you want us to send Dewi and Gwen out,' she asks.

'No, it's okay,' says Alis. 'I'm only telling the truth.'

She looks from me to Dewi and says, 'they forced me to go up the chimney. They said only I could fit and they said I had to see how far up I could get.'

Dewi and I are holding hands under the table. I don't know how it happened or why, but we're gripping each other's hand so hard that it's painful and I think we must be bracing ourselves. When we have a conference we aren't allowed to speak until it's our turn, but I am bursting to stand up and argue. I manage to resist but Dewi does not.

'Lies,' he says, banging his free hand on the table. 'She went up herself. We told her not to. She's always doing crazy stuff, especially in the other-house when she thinks you can't see her.'

'Since Dewi thinks it's okay to shout out, I will hear from Gwen next,' says Mam. She looks tired today. Dark circles around her eyes make the delicate skin there look sunken.

'Dewi is right,' I say. 'She's wild. We were just following her. She likes going in there a lot on her own. She doesn't seem to be scared at all.'

'They're lying,' says Alis in a loud voice, and then she bursts into tears.

'There, there,' I say, standing and reaching my hand across to pat her shoulder. I think this will look good.

'Get off!' she says and shrugs me away.

'Well if we don't get the truth out of them, perhaps they can all be punished,' says Tad. He looks livid. I like that word. It's a bit like liquid.

'We haven't heard everything yet,' says Mam. She is trying hard to be calm, I can tell. Just like me. I've got one foot on top of the other, pressing down hard and have let go of Dewi's hand to grip my chair instead as if to keep myself on it.

'How did you end up trapped in the chest?'

'It was them who decided to play hide and seek,' says Alis. 'By then I was filthy and just wanted to go back and try and get clean. I thought the chest would be a good hiding place, even though I didn't want to play. Gwen was with me when I got in. I thought she would get in too, but she said there wasn't room. Then she shut the lid on me and that was when she must have put the catch on to stop me getting out. I didn't realise straight away. I waited and waited but no one came to find me. Gwen knew where I was, but she must have thought it a good joke to leave me there all alone—'

'No,' I say. 'It was your idea to play hide and seek and I didn't put the catch on. I didn't even know there was a catch!'

'Have I asked you to speak?' asks Tad, with that look of disgust on his face again.

I try to wipe the moustache, I can feel the makeup beneath my nose, a funny coated feeling, all shiny and heavy.

'I'm thinking that it might be better to get their stories out of them separately this time,' says Mam. 'I don't want any collusion. What do you think?'

'Yes, I agree,' says Tad. 'I'll take Dewi out. You stay here with these two. Come on, son.'

As Tad rises from the table I stare at Dewi with my strobe eyes and send out power from my witch necklace. I try to get the message to him. Our agreement. Be confident. Don't give in. Dewi glances at me before following Tad out of the kitchen. I notice that he is still wearing my skirt, but he has tucked it into his trousers.

*

Mam has gone from reasonable and patient to angry and exasperated and back again. Ex-as-per-ate-ed. I have held fast to my story and Alis to hers. I don't know who Mam suspects. Maybe she should just give up now and accept the truth. We are all liars. She's talking all soft to me now, this reminds me of my teacher, who uses the same tactics.

'—tell the truth and there will be no consequences. For the next five minutes I give you an amnesty, both of you. You will not be punished. But after that, if your father and I have to keep on at you, and we will, until we get to the bottom of this— we will be angry at all the wasted time and I can assure you that you will be punished to the degree that you deserve.'

I notice that as she speaks, she spends most of her time looking at me and not Alis. It's annoying that she appears to suspect me more. Just because Alis is the youngest doesn't mean she's always innocent. Far from it, I'd say.

'Well, would either of you like to give me the true story?'

Mam's voice goes up a little at the end of that sentence and I hear the tension and exasperation in there. That's right Mam, I think, it's all a story and forget the truth. I wonder if she's just as much a liar as we are. Will she go back on the amnesty as soon as she gets what she wants? I look at Alis. Is she about to crack? No, she looks as if she's half-smiling. Can't think why though. I look down into the fire grate at the peat smoking there and push my feet towards the warmth. I consider the amnesty. I also consider a favourite trick of the experienced liar: admitting to part of what I did while continuing to vehemently deny the rest. But which bit to admit to? The least harmful bit of course. The only problem is that Dewi might be telling a whole different story.

I look up at Mam. Her eyes are on me. Intense.

'I do have something to admit,' I say.

'Oh. Do tell,' says Mam.

'And the amnesty is still on?' I ask.

'Yes of course.'

'This is what I've been hiding.'

'Carry on.'

'I don't know how Alis got to be in the other-house after we went to bed last night but Dewi and I looked for her this morning. And while you were out, we found her naked and covered in poo and dirt. She pooed all over herself. I am guilty of hiding this from you. We—well mostly me—had to clean her up—.'

'Liar!' shouts Alis.

'No,' I say. 'And you know it. This is the truth.' I turn to Mam. 'I didn't want you and Tad to see her in that state.'

'Liar,' says Alis in an angry voice, although some of the power of her denial has gone.

'Maybe we'll find your dirty clothes somewhere then you won't be able to deny it,' I say.

Alis blushes. 'You only cleaned me so you could try and get me to not tell on you,' she says.

I look at Mam, 'sounds like she's admitted to that at least,' I say.

'So it does,' says Mam. Her face is a suspicious frown.

Alis starts to cry. 'I couldn't help it. They locked me in the chest.'

'No,' I say. 'As I said before, I didn't even see the catch. You must have gone back into the house later and locked yourself in somehow. Why can't you get it into your thick head that you must have done it yourself?'

'That's enough Gwen,' says Mam. 'No name-calling.'

'Mam, I don't think you're going to get the truth this time as Alis seems convinced that I locked her in and left her. She has no evidence but she wants to think that. I know for a fact that I never saw or moved a catch and as far as I knew she was in bed.'

'I'm more bothered about answering this question,' says Mam. 'Did you and Dewi leave Alis behind in the upstairs of the main house?'

I look her in the eye and think of an actress on the stage. I raise my chin like Vivien Leigh and I let my eyes blaze with indignation.

'We did not. She was with us.'

'Liar,' says Alis.

'Is that all you can say?'

I fancy that word carries less weight now.

'You have sleepwalked before,' says Mam in a soothing voice as she turns to Alis.

'I *know* what happened,' says Alis indignantly. 'Gwen is lying.'

Mam looks back at me but before she can open her mouth to continue with the interrogation, the door opens behind us and I feel the cold draught on my back as Dewi and Tad come back in. I hardly dare, but I have to look. At first, I can't see Dewi because he's walking rather sheepishly behind Tad. Then I see the slumped shoulders and the red crying face. Sometimes he calls me baby crier, but I think he cries more. He just tries to hide it from Tad because then he gets a lecture about being a man. I can't imagine that Dewi will ever be a man, he's so skinny in his arms and legs and he likes wearing my skirts. But the crying isn't a good sign. Maybe it's all over, maybe Tad has broken him. I sit up straight like Tad tells me to. A straight back is a sign of a person in control of themselves, he says. I attempt to look innocent without looking like I'm acting, I've been caught out a few times that way, but a person learns. I try to catch Dewi's eye but he doesn't even look at me, not a good sign either.

'Well,' asks Mam. 'What did he have to say for himself?'

'Couldn't get much sense out of him,' said Tad. 'Cried like a girl.'

I give Tad my most indignant look. Am I crying?

'He's saying they definitely brought Alis back here and that she's created a drama to get attention.'

Tad looks at Alis after these words.

'Not true,' she protests. 'They're lying. They always lie.'

I detect a little less vehemence in her despite her protest and I wonder if Dewi and I are close to being off the hook.

'Perhaps we'll discuss this somewhere else,' says Mam. 'You three stay in here and no more arguing. You father and I will discuss what's been said and what to do next. We may have to have another conference.'

We all say nothing, but watch them go.

'Can't we just have some peace now?' I ask no one in particular. 'At this rate I'll tell them that I'm happy to take the blame for everything. Yes, even the Second World War, I'll take the blame for that too. Just so we don't have to sit in another conference.'

'You weren't born till 1943, so that's not possible,' says Dewi with a laugh.

'Well at least my face isn't all puffy from crying. Baby crier.'

'Shut up,' says Dewi.

I look at Alis, she has gone quiet. I want to make amends; the guilt I feel is becoming a heavy burden.

'Alis, can we put an end to all this?' I ask. 'Can we not make peace? Adults make war, not kids.'

Alis gives me her dirtiest look. 'Why should I want to speak to either of you ever again?' she says. 'But maybe—if you tell the truth.'

'The amnesty is over,' I say. 'And I did tell the truth.'

'Only one part of it, the part that makes me look bad.'

'Well, I think we'll just have to agree to disagree because Dewi and I brought you back and that is the story we are sticking with because it's true.' I look at Dewi as I say this.

Now Dewi tries: 'Alis, sometimes people see things differently. We all think we're telling some sort of truth, but maybe the truth is something none of us know. I mean the real truth.'

'Yes,' I say. 'Maybe you were concussed or sleep-walking again and somehow you've got dreams and real life muddled.' As I say this, it occurs to me that I could have banged her on the head like they do in films, then she'd really have a concussion and might not remember. It isn't the first time that I've thought of this although films make it look easy and I worry that I wouldn't hit her hard enough and it wouldn't work and then she'd have another reason to tell on me.

Alis sighs. 'I'm fed up of this too. I want it to go away.'

There is of course also the chance that I'd hit her too hard and kill her by accident.

'Have you still got my necklace?' she asks.

'It's not yours,' I say. 'You had the bracelet.'

'That's not fair,' says Alis. 'You took the brooch too.'

'Well they're gone now. Mam has them. I'll give you a doll for the necklace.'

'Do I get to choose which one?' she asks.

'Er, no. But they're all nice. Is it a deal?'

She nods and we shake on it. Then I put my hand on top of hers. 'Let's be friends again.' I give Dewi the look.

Dewi, with a bit of reluctance, places his hand on top of Alis's and mine.

'Friends,' he says.

We look at Alis expectantly. She takes her time, but finally looks at both of us with a half-smile.

'I don't want to move away from this house,' she says.

'Neither do I.'

'I hid from you all, that's why you couldn't find me.'

She smiles to herself. I want to ask her where she hid but before I can open my mouth she speaks for me.

'Our secret,' she says and then: 'Can I play with your dolls?'

'Well I'm giving you one of them, but yes, you can,' I say. 'Just tell Mam and Tad that you think you must have been sleep-walking. It's the only explanation that can sort this mess out.'

Alis considers this and then gives the slightest nod. In a minute we will all start talking and it will feel like a weight has been lifted. We will make plans to play games and do fun things together as a threesome. We will be careful not to argue or be mean. It'll be what I always call the golden period. I know already that it won't last long, but we'll try our best to make it last a few days, maybe even a week or two. In the end, the goodness always runs out. For now at this moment, we have all our hands clasped together and it's the start. We're all smiling at each other. It's so beautiful that I want to cry. Dewi and I have Alis's hand and also with our other hands, we've given each other the victory handshake under the table; but Alis doesn't see that.

24

It's our last day of living at Gwylfa Hiraethog and Dewi has found something else slotted into the wall, where he found the photograph. I have joined him, sitting on his bed. Almost everything is packed except for the things we are leaving behind. I'm glad of something to distract me from the sadness I feel.

'It's a letter,' he says.

I take the envelope from him gently because it looks old and fragile. The paper feels brittle and is yellow as if it was wet at one time. It says 'Dora' on the envelope, but underneath it there's also a letter 'B'.

'It's a love letter,' I say, after I've read it and I watch Dewi do his usual fake vomiting. 'Two people called Dora and Owen, who must have been in love.'

'A long time ago,' says Dewi. 'Look at the date.'

'1914,' I say. 'That is quite old, but they could still be alive.'

'First World War started that year,' says Dewi.

'I don't understand why there was a photo of Beryl hidden with it,' I say.

'Well it does have a 'B' on it.'

'Shall we show Mam?' I wonder. 'She might know the names.'

'If you do, she will take it off you. She always goes on about things being important historical artefacts and then she goes and gives them away and we never see them again.'

'She gave the coins to the museum, so maybe we could see them if we went there.'

'I say keep it. It's falling apart anyway. No one would want it.'

'Okay. We could put it in that tin box that we found the witch jewellery in.'

'Yes.'

*

My dearest,

I have tried to write many times over the years that I've known you but nothing was good enough to send. I hope that this letter gets to you as I destroyed all the others. I am not a very good writer. I have written this many times, just to get to this version.

You were right in your letter to me, I was disappointed when you did not tell your brother that day and instead, you denied what we were to each other. I thought that was our chance to begin to tell the world, but now I see that it was too soon for you. I still want to believe that you will stand up and tell the truth about us one day, like you said you would. It is thanks to you that I have found the strength in me. I cannot think of a better woman to have in my life than one who is as courageous as you are. So don't fret my dear, your letter made me sad as you were too hard on yourself. I can forgive all of that easily now, and I want you to know that I still love you.

I must go off to fight now. As you know, I am not really the fighting kind but my father says we all must do our part.

Yesterday, I visited Gwylfa and the moor. I did not go in to the house, though I looked up at your bedroom window as I passed as if I hoped to see you there. I did not want to talk with anyone except for you, nor did anyone see me there. I went to the place where we last met and stayed there a while, thinking of how to write to you and what to say. I closed my eyes and remembered how it was that day. It brought tears. Then it started raining and still I sat there. I stayed until I was soaked. I kept looking out for you, as if I could make you real by wishing. I did not see the Roman centurion, so do not worry about that.

It seems to be a hopeless dream, yet I still cling on to the dream of us. It really only exists in our minds as it is. I haven't known what to do since you did not come this summer. It is not your fault I know that. I thought to come down there to find you, but there is no time now. If I return from this war, I will find you again.

Some doubts do trouble me, and I wonder if you will have forgotten me, or if they have found you another suitor who is better for you. I hear stories and I don't know what to believe.

I will return to Gwylfa tomorrow to hide this letter there and hope that you will find it. I will ask Dora to help.

Know that I am still yours to this day and all the days that come after.

Yours with all my love,
Owen.

*

Dewi and I are in the playroom with Alis and we've decided to go on an adventure for our last day here.

'We will make a box of secrets to bury,' I say. 'In it I have put the letter and photo that Dewi found in the wall. What else can we put in?'

'That witch necklace you wear,' says Dewi.

'No, I'm keeping that, but I'll put the hair inside it in there, because I don't want that.'

We go off to find or make things to leave as treasure. Alis draws pictures of the three of us and writes the year beneath them. She adds some of the bits of Gwylfa that she has collected. Dewi has put in the skull of a bird that he found on the moor and a girl figure from his farm set because he says he doesn't like girl things. I just raise my eyebrows at that.

Soon, we have quite a collection. We can't stop now that we've started.

'I'll put this in,' says Alis.

She drops the black bracelet in.

'How did you get that?' I ask.

'I stole it back from Mam. Stealing is easy.'

She smiles her wicked little smile.

'What about the brooch?'

'I've got that too, but I'm keeping that. You have the necklace, so I get to keep the brooch.'

'That's fair,' I say, and as I look down at the objects in the box, something makes me pick up the envelope with the letter inside. I put the lock of black hair and the photo of Beryl inside the envelope with the letter, and carefully roll it up. Then I wrap the black bracelet around it.

'Come one then, let's go,' I say.

*

In our warmest coats, we venture out. Dewi and I have our bobble hats on to match our sister. Nain knitted ours too. It is not a bad day, there is no wind, and a watery sun. Mam is stripping our beds and glad to have us out of the way. We follow a path, crunchy with old snow that has been frozen, but it's now shrinking as it melts, and Alis whinges about not wanting to move away.

'I don't want to go either,' I say, looking back at the house with its dark paintless walls and damaged roof. 'It looks like a scary old haunted house, but it's our home.'

Dewi nods, 'I don't really want anyone else to live there either. It feels like it should still be ours. Our new house is so small compared to Gwylfa.'

We continue on the path, until the house looks distant. Dewi carries a spade and I have a trowel. We took them without asking from a wooden box in the hallway. I hated seeing all those boxes lined up, ready to leave.

'We have to find somewhere with deeper soil,' I say, 'not a rocky place or we won't be able to bury it.'

'Look for marsh grass then,' says Dewi. 'Bogs are deep so boggy places are best.'

'I'm not going in a bog and drowning,' says Alis.

'Well, we're just looking for soil not an actual bog,' I say.

We are silent for a few seconds as we follow the sheep path.

'You never did tell us where you hid your dirty clothes,' says Dewi suddenly, turning to look at Alis.

'It's a secret,' she says.

'Promise I won't tell.'

'I'll tell you after we've moved out,' she says.

'Look, what about here?' I ask.

There is marsh grass and a high bank, followed by a drop down. Beneath the bank is a small stone wall in a horseshoe shape. There are many of these on the moors.

'What are all these walls anyway?'

Dewi shrugs. 'Probably witch places for spells and all that.'

'Try digging,' I say. 'You're the oldest.'

He scrapes the snow away and throws the spade into the ground, in a rather unskilful manner but it goes in about an inch quite easily.

'This'll do,' he says and lifts it again, a bit more accurately this time, mimicking how Tad cuts the peat.

The wall behind this area is tumbling down, the stones covered by moss, lichen and the marsh grass which threatens to overgrow everything. I look across the moor and see that the heather is starting to poke up through the melting snow. When Dewi stops to rest, I take the spade and continue, handing the trowel to Alis, who helps, while also trying to avoid my vicious thrusts with the spade.

'This is harder than I expected,' says Alis.

'We don't have to go down far,' says Dewi.

'As long as we don't ever murder anyone, we'll be okay,' I say. 'Imagine how deep down you would have to go to bury a whole body.'

'You could chop it into bits to make it easier,' says Dewi. 'That's what proper murderers do.'

After we've dug down deep enough, we try the box and dig a bit more until it fits. Before we bury it, we open it and arrange everything neatly, with the secret letter and bracelet in the middle. Then we do a dance around it. Eira and I call it a magic fairy dance and Dewi joins in without any complaint. We go round and round three times clockwise and three times anti-clockwise. After burying the box we break off tough marsh grass that slips through our hands, so that we have to bend and rip it, and then we place it over the little earth mound before piling snow on top. Eira brings some stones out of her pocket, though as I get a closer look, I see that they are bits of Gwylfa, cracked bits of plaster, stone and brick. We arrange these in a circle on top of the snow.

When we are satisfied we walk back to the house, although I dawdle off the path and find a skull in the heather. I call the others over.

'What is it?' asks Alis.

'It looks like a dog,' I say.

'Fox, more like,' says Dewi. 'They die of starvation in the winter.'

'I hope Tad didn't kill it,' I say, unsure.

Dewi reaches down to touch the skull.

'You shouldn't touch dead things,' says Alis, before touching it herself.

Dewi ignores her and picks up the skull.

'Mam and Tad won't let you take that to the new house,' I say.

'Maybe not,' he says, 'but they can't stop me taking something small.'

He bends down and puts his foot on it, while pulling at one of the long, canine teeth. It is not difficult to remove. He removes three and hands one to Alis and me. 'For good luck,' he says. 'Make sure you hide them.'

25

February 1955

The gas lights have been lit for the last time. The snow has melted, replaced by dark clouds, puddles and grey rain. The Thomas family have moved out. Ghastly pranks and voices raised in defiant anger will not be missed, but the soft, slippered feet on stairs, the gentle touch of a mittened hand on old handles followed by the determined pushing at swollen doors, unsticking them, letting air flow through, will be lamented. Sometimes in the night Alis would croon to her stuffed toys, quite tunefully, and her mother hummed and sang as she sewed. The little noises and the small gestures, and the ticking of a life within. A house hunkers down against wind and rain.

But here comes someone. Though the sky is darkening, a man comes with a bag and tools. He unloads a ladder and climbs onto my roof. His boots are heavy and he grunts in a beastly way as he climbs and he curses without restraint. It is long overdue, slipped tiles need replacing and a few are missing altogether. Inside timbers are getting wet and beginning to rot. It is time for repairs. The man does not bring any tiles, but tools for extraction. He looks about frequently as if he expects some ghost to appear from behind. He is not here to make repairs. He is a thief here to steal the lead that protects my roof. Hudson's lead, chosen because it was one of the most durable and reliable roofing materials. This roof might have lasted two hundred years if it had been cared for. This is excruciating. Where is help to be found?

The man works, taking away the lead an armful at a time and returning for more. He concentrates on the section over the dining room, facing south and sheltered from the wind. A few hours pass and he does not stop, except to wipe the sweat from his face. This section of roof looks as if it has been hit by a hurricane. His breath is fast and ragged and he frequently looks about. Once he has loosened the tiles, he kicks them off with his boots; they crash noisily to the floor below. A few vehicles have passed by far below on the A543, too far away to see what is happening. Now he is throwing the lead off the roof too. With a new urgency he attacks; he wants this work to finish soon.

'Hey there! You!' The voice sounds distant but the wind carries it close.

The thief curses loudly and attempts to pull his cap down over his eyes to camouflage himself, but a gust of wind blows it off and it falls off the roof, just as its owner now half falls, half climbs down, dropping most of the precious lead as he goes. It falls to the ground and he chooses to leave most of it there. He runs, holding as much as he can carry along with his tools, breathless, grunting, swearing, but he will not escape. They know who he is and have picked up his hat.

26

Hudson

October 1924

'Better you than me,' says Mrs Hughes. 'Don't get me wrong, it's a beautiful house; but it must be so much work to look after all these big houses. You're a brave man Viscount.'

'I have two houses,' I say. 'Not two dozen. Though I admit I've got my eye on an estate in Scotland.'

I'm sitting with Beryl and Mark at our customary table in the Crown Hotel. Mrs Hughes has joined us. She always gives me a slug of whisky in my coffee—on the house. She says it'll keep me warm for the journey.

'Anyway, this time is different,' I tell her. 'Gwylfa is going up for sale.'

When she's gotten over the surprise, Mrs Hughes purses her lips and says: 'I thought you were visiting rather later than usual.'

'Just tying up loose ends.'

'Is this why Gerald hasn't accompanied you?'

'Yes, Gerald isn't keen to see it go.'

'I will certainly miss seeing you.'

'I expect we'll still visit,' I say. 'I've become quite attached to this area and have made many friends here.'

'I'm glad to hear it,' she says. 'I trust retirement is treating you well? You look more rested these days.'

'I retired seven years ago,' I remind her. 'I'm getting old, Mrs Hughes. I will turn seventy in just two years.'

She grimaces, perhaps it wasn't the answer she wanted. After all, when I first came here thirty years ago, I was a whirlwind of a man with ambitious plans. Gwylfa is still the highest inhabited house in Wales at 1,627 feet, but it's time to let it go. I feel rather like the curtains of the Crown Hotel, a bit old and faded.

We're eating our traditional poached egg followed by scones with rhubarb jam. Rhubarb is very popular in these parts. Beryl and Mark used to get so excited about the travelling, they aren't children anymore of course, both are past thirty.

'I have many good memories of your time here.' Mrs Hughes is saying. 'One of my favourites is when Lloyd George visited and gave us a little speech at the railway station, before he went up to stay with you. He was probably the greatest Prime Minister this country will ever see. He had the tongue of a dragon.'

I notice that she speaks of him in the past tense.

'Dei is finished in politics, though he doesn't know it yet,' I concede. 'He can at least look back and see that his powers, which were considerable, were well-spent.'

'Maybe it's time for him to retire and enjoy life more.'

'I think he's got a bit more fight in him yet though.'

'Yes,' she says. 'He's a fighter if I ever saw one. Led us through the war and ousted a Prime Minister who got in the way, but then Asquith probably needed to go.'

'Dei never wanted to oust Asquith,' I say. 'He did a lot to avoid that, even stepping down from Chancellor to a lower job in the war. Even when Asquith was forced out, Dei told me he hadn't wanted the premiership, just to be in charge of the war effort.'

'Ah,' says Mrs Hughes. 'Then it wasn't exactly how the papers reported it,'

'Indeed, the papers cannot seem to report anything accurately these days,' I say. 'All governments are full of Iagos, whispering poison. Lesser men usually. I know from my own experience. I suppose it is easy enough to pin a crime onto someone you don't like and there were many who disliked him. There's a lot of jealousy and petty mindedness in politics. I found it shocking at times to hear of ridiculous little battles and scores being settled by grown men, while outside in the real world we were at war and men were dying in the trenches. But none of those lesser creatures will be remembered in the end. I made myself ill in the war, working hard to set up that Ministry of Food, but it only took a few newspapers to make it look as if I never did anything of use. Well drat them all, I say.'

Mrs Hughes looks horrified and veers off into family matters. She wants to know if Beryl has met anyone new since her last beau.

'I have no interest,' says Beryl with a shake of her head.

Mark changes the subject.

'Gwylfa should sell quite fast. It's a fantastic estate. I see it as a fine country hotel in the future.'

'No,' says Mrs Hughes. 'You forget that it would only be habitable for about five months of the year unless you can find a market for gale-force winds and thick fog. Or perhaps guests who like blizzards and being snowed in for weeks on end. No, it just wouldn't make money.'

Mark frowns at this unwanted Welsh honesty. Mrs Hughes blushes and suddenly notices there are dishes that need clearing from another table.

It is probably the first time that we've come here without something new for Gwylfa, some trinket or item of use that we thoughtfully reserved. Offerings. One year a fine croquet set, another year a set of purple curtains for Beryl's room, and just two years ago a bear rug from Nova Scotia. Now the house has become a burden. There is difficulty in getting the staff to look after it. Odd when you think of how much easier it is to get up there now in modern motors, yet people are different now too.

It's raining today and as our motor chugs up the moor road, the views are obscured, rather like the day when the Norwegians began erecting the first version of the house.

I can see it now, the road that winds around Hiraethog allows a distant view. It isn't a particularly good view as the house appears and disappears behind a shifting fog. My heart always beats a little faster at the first sight of it, but the thrill is now replaced by doubt.

'Hubris,' they said.
'English fool.'
'The wind will knock it down.'

The English fool is back. We lose the view of it for a time, until we're close, then it materialises, quite menacingly. The lighthouse paint we used to seal its walls will need redoing before long. And it leaks in places, even after the rebuild.

I am suddenly overcome by sadness. For a moment I search around for the source of this melancholy; it's as if someone else's grief has descended upon me. I take in a huge gulp of air that is more like the beginning of a sob and realise that I'm on the verge of tears. I close my eyes and try to calm down. I have been ill, but remind myself that I have recovered. When I open my eyes again, the house is before us as my driver takes the final off-road track up to the front door. Beryl pats my arm.

'Are you ready?'

'Yes.'

*

With just two members of staff to look after us and the house on this occasion, I'm impressed by their efficiency and wonder why we once needed so many. We've eaten well and are playing cards until the rain clears. Beyond the heavy drapes, the moor is lost in a thick fog.

'On a clear day you can see forever, but in all twenty-eight years of owning this house, I can only recall three occasions when it was really clear,' I say. 'We were able to see the Mourne Mountains in Ulster on all three occasions.'

'The Isle of Man too,' says Beryl.

'And just once we think we saw the Mull of Galloway which is about a hundred miles away.'

'There have been many more clear days than that,' says Mark.

'Ah yes, but those three days were exceptional,' I rejoinder. 'Each time we had extraordinary visibility and each time there was a southwest gale straight after.'

Mark smiles. I know he thinks I'm talking nonsense.

'Let's take a walk,' says Beryl.

Mark declines. He has his easel and oils out and wants to be alone for one last painting of the house.

It is clearer by the time we venture out. Our walking pace is evenly matched.

'You can come out of mourning now, Beryl,' I say as we follow the sheep path through the drizzle. 'I don't like seeing you in black all the time; it's been years.'

Beryl sighs. Her arm is linked through mine but weighs heavily.

'I'll always be in mourning,' she says. 'I quite like black and have got used to it. But I might stop wearing it all the time, just for you Papa. Anyway, look I've changed my locket for a blue one at least.'

'But you're still wearing the black bracelet,' I say. 'And that rather macabre brooch.'

'I'll stop wearing the mourning jewellery. You're right. It has done its part in reminding me.'

'We were lucky to get the boys back at least,' I say. 'If one of them had fallen—well I daren't think of it. And it was a terrible shame about that boy, what was his name again?'

'Owen,' she says.

'Can't have been older than twenty—.'

'He was twenty six, Papa. He died at Messines, the same as Jonathan.'

'You remember him well.'

'He did work for us Papa; his father too.'

She smiles, but it's strained and her eyes look sparkly as if there are tears crowding in.

'That poor father,' I say. 'He'll be old now, if he is still alive. To outlive your own child, I can't imagine that pain, though I've had many occasions to observe it in others.'

Beryl squeezes my arm, and I see that she is in tears.

'Oh my dear,' I say. 'I'm sorry to have reminded you.'

'It's alright, Papa,' she says, though her voice is choked and I can tell she is struggling to hold back a torrent of grief.

'Let it out dear,' I say. 'Don't repress it.'

She leans on me and sobs, poor thing. There is nothing I can say or do. I can only hold her and be there. As she cries, memories of Owen return to me. I recall that she had a liking for the boy when he worked for us and I had to forbid them from speaking to each other. Later, Mark claimed there had been something going on there for years, but by that time the boy had enlisted and gone to fight. I had no stomach to hear tales then, yet I wonder now at this outpouring of grief. Who is it for? There is no anger left in me, whatever the answer. I only wish for her to be happier than she is, I would let her marry whoever she wants now, but I do not say this. It would be of no help.

'You should go to more parties,' I say, when she has recovered somewhat. 'I'm sure there are many men—'

'Papa, no, please. I'm not interested now. It was hard enough to find Johnathan and—I don't know if I like men that much. Except for you of course.'

'You're too young to give up.'

'I like being an independent lady.'

'I don't like to think of you alone.'

'I'm not. I have lots of girl-friends, and memories to keep me entertained.'

'Don't talk of memories. You still have so much ahead of you. It will get easier. Your greatest days are yet to come.'

'What were your greatest days, Papa?' she asks and I'm saddened to see her tear-streaked face. I decide it is best to try and distract her.

Yet, I cannot answer for a while, even though I know the answer really. We follow the narrow path through the heather to a small lake and stand near it in the gloom.

'Why is this here anyway?' she asks.

'It's a small quarry. There are a few in this area.'

'Oh, yes. I thought it might be.'

Somewhere to the north, a curlew cries.

'My hey-day was being secretary to the President of the Board of Trade when Dei took the presidency. You three were all young children and I had many plans. Dei came into that office and turned it around. His methods weren't always the most honest, he knew how to play one group off against another and was a master manipulator, but it was all for a good cause. Those days burned bright.'

'What else?'

'My work at the Port of London, I feel proud that I set it all up from scratch.'

'I wonder how different it would have been if you had been in the cabinet like Lloyd George wanted.'

'I can hardly imagine that now.'

'Perhaps you could have saved the Liberal party.'

'I doubt it. Dei has a lot to answer for there, although perhaps he doesn't realise. He was too far to the left and too radical for much of the party in peacetime, and when war broke out, he went too far the other way.'

'He didn't fit in then.'

'He didn't play the politician's game but was led by his own conscience. A policy was weighed for its value to society instead of its value in gaining votes and support. He was not without passion, whatever his faults.'

'Do you think the liberal party can regain greatness?'

'I'm not sure it can. It was divided for a long time, but I think we saw the end when the Asquithians refused reconciliation with Lloyd George.'

She squeezes my arm.

'What about Gwylfa? Will anyone buy it?'

'It depends if there is another mad Englishman. The Welsh won't.'

We stare at the lake for a while, perhaps she is watching how it is pitted by rain as I am. I think of another time when we two stood here together. It was night on that occasion; the night of a party thrown for Dei and Maggie.

*

The September air was cool but the sky was clear. Beryl was around twenty then.

She had dragged me outside to look at the meagre light of pin-prick stars. I was due to make a short speech to guests and a toast to Dei. I was never a great speaker myself. I was always a man of business, but I did my duty. Dei always said I was a great organiser.

Beryl was telling me how to find the North Star as we walked to the small lake. She was insistent about a moonlit walk, but no one wanted to leave the lights and gaiety of the house, so I went. In those days she reminded me of my younger self. Full of life and energy.

Earlier that night, when darkness had only just closed over the moor and the lamps were lit, I had danced with my daughter, noticing her like never before. Small jewels glittered in her upswept hair which had gained a lustrous shine under the chandelier. She danced well, thanks to that Swiss finishing school Selina had insisted upon. They said she was most like me in temper. She wore a yellow dress that skimmed the floor, or was it blue? She was graceful, though her frame was that of her mother, strong and upright, a dominant young woman. She often outclassed opponents of the other sex with her quick tongue. I thought then that she'd make a fine politician; in a time when women would be allowed that. Yet that night I saw another side, the glitter in her dark eyes as she danced and laughed and whirled her old father about the room, she was entertaining and vivacious. She pulled her brothers out one after the other and made them dance. She was shyer about dancing with Dei, but he was always a gentleman with her. He had a reputation, but I saw only sadness in his eyes as he looked at her. She beat him at chess, she was a good player. They got on well, but the only man she ever had eyes for was Johnathan. Yet I cannot see his face, when I try to remember him. Instead, that boy Owen appears in my mind. Handsome chap, dark-haired like his father with his mother's good looks. He was a good worker, I remember little else. I look at my daughter, and worry that she will always be alone now.

'Where are you now, Papa?'

Beryl's voice brings me back to the present, standing by the small lake. I see her concerned look, the age lines forming around her dark eyes and on each side of her mouth. I wonder how she sees me.

'Come on, Papa,' she says, 'lunch.'

I use my stick to help me back to cucumber sandwiches and a pot of tea. Mark abandons his painting on our return. He has not quite finished, but he has created a fine depiction of the views through the window of the dining room. It's a little more abstract than his earlier style. The earthy tones show the browns and russets of the October heather rather well.

Later, as Mark and Beryl rummage for the chess board, I remain sitting in the drawing room and look out at the coveted view. I am reminded of the day that Dei named the house for me. We were rambling over the moors just before sunset, talking passionately about politics as usual. It was as we walked back to the house and it loomed above us against a glowing backdrop that he stopped suddenly.

'Gwylfa Hiraethog,' he said.

'What does that mean?' I asked.

'It's what you should call the house. Gwylfa means watchtower. Hiraethog is harder to explain.'

Dei turned and pointed vaguely at the expanse of heather and sky.

'The closest English words are nostalgia—and longing.'

'Ah.'

'You do know that they are right in what they say, don't you?'

'What about?'

'The wind will knock it down.'

27

THE RESIDENCE:
"GWYLFA HIRAETHOG"
Parish of Bylchau

Built with local stone and cement faced with Gwespyr stone dressings. The acclaimed architect Edwin Cooper, commissioned by the owner, Viscount Devonport, designed this Jacobean-style mansion. At 1,627 feet above sea level, this sportsman's mansion is situated in a most beautiful and healthy part of North Wales, with far-reaching 360-degree views of the Hiraethog Mountain and the national park of Snowdonia.

A carriage drive leads from the Denbigh to Pentrefoelas road up to the front door in the eastern elevation. The accommodation comprises:

ON THE GROUND FLOOR:

VESTIBULE and OUTER HALL, each having a heavy, oak panelled door and an open fireplace with fine-looking stone mantel.

INNER STAIRCASE HALL leading to:

DINING ROOM, 24ft 6ins x 17ft, with striking oak mantelpiece.

DRAWING ROOM, 23ft 6ins extending to 30ft 6ins into Annexe x 21ft wide.

MORNINGROOM or LIBRARY/STUDY, 19ft 6ins x 15ft

CLOAKROOM, fitted with ornate lavatory and sanitary convenience.
GUNROOM, etc.

ON THE FIRST FLOOR:

ELEVEN PRINCIPAL BEDROOMS, two dressing rooms, two secondary bedrooms, three bathrooms (with two ornate lavatories), separate lavatory, heated linen cupboard, etc.
NOTE: Two bedrooms, a dressing room, a bathroom, and a separate lavatory, all *en-suite*, are entirely shut off from the main landing.

THE DOMESTIC OFFICES:

The service section on the North side of the mansion is extensive and complete, comprising kitchen, back kitchen, larder, butler's pantry, beer cellar, storerooms, housekeeper's rooms, servants' hall and fitted drying room; also, approached by two separate stairways are SIX BEDROOMS.

THE OUTBUILDINGS:

Heating chamber, engine house, petrol store, game store, and shed, which could be adapted for use as a garage. There is also a good range of four dog kennels with ornate metalwork and yards, situated a convenient distance from the house.

THE PROPERTY BENEFITS FROM:

LIGHTING Petrol vapour gas which produces a light equal to electric and which is generated on a system installed by the Loco Vapour Gas Company of Manchester.

CENTRAL HEATING throughout, with radiators in all parts of the house.

WATER is pumped to two large storage tanks in the roof of the house by a "ram" (by James Keith of London and Edinburgh). There is also a subsidiary supply from a spring well with a Petter Oil Engine and Pump (1922 model), so that a plentiful supply of water is always assured. Hot water is supplied by a separate boiler, independent of the kitchen range.

DRAINAGE to a cesspool. This excellent system is in good order with ample inspection chambers.

THE GROUSE MOOR AND SHOOTING RIGHTS:

THE GROUSE MOOR, known as BRYN TRILLYN, with the moorland farms adjoining, is of a total acreage of 322 acres, and forms one of the best moors in North Wales. It is well drained, the heather is in excellent condition, whinberries provide attractive feeding, and it is mainly free from sheep. The land has been shot by the Vendor in conjunction with the extensive areas adjoining, which he holds on lease on terms as follows:-

The Shooting over the Crown Lands contiguous to the Gwylfa Estate embraces an area of over 7,000 acres, held under Lease which will expire in April 1929, at a rental of £235 per annum. Viscount Devonport has sported over these lands continuously for thirty years and (additionally) he has shooting leases over a further area of about 5,000 acres, rented from the Birkenhead Corporation at a rental of £284 per annum, which expire in February 1929.

The bags from the whole area have aggregated, in good years, from 500 to 700 brace of Grouse. There is also good Duck, Snipe and Wild Fowl Shooting.

THE SPORTSMAN'S ARMS:

Together with the land known as **BRYN TRILLYN FARM**, containing a total area of 33 acres or thereabouts, now in the occupation of Mr Issac Evans at the nominal rental of £50 per annum, upon a tenancy from year to year, subject to twelve months' notice.

THE HOUSE comprises porch entrance, tap-room, dining-room, kitchen and larder on the ground floor, with four bedrooms and a storeroom above, and a beer cellar in the basement. The whole of the ground floor is fully licensed for the sale of beer, wines, spirits and tobacco.

THE FARM BUILDINGS comprise three three-stalled stables, shippon to tie five cows, small barn, double cart shed, pigsty, fowl houses, etc., grouped around a large central yard.

GARAGE a stone-built, slated garage, used by the Vendor.

The LAND is all good pasture land.

TITHE RENT amounting to about £3 1s 8d per annum on this lot, together with the land held with **GWYLFA HIRAETHOG**.

Also included in the estate:

CWM-Y-RHINWEDD FARM

Containing an area of 66 acres 3 roods 14 perches or thereabouts, is in the occupation of Miss Evans upon an annual tenancy.

BRYN-EITHIN AND AFON UCHA FARMS

Containing an area of 63 acres, 2 roods 27 perches or thereabouts, are in the occupation of Mr Hugh Evans upon an annual tenancy.

GENERAL REMARKS:

GWYLFA HIRAETHOG, although entirely surrounded by moorland, has the great advantage of being easily accessible by a first-class road. The scenery over the mountain and sea is magnificent, and so extensive in its range that Ireland, Scotland and the Isle of Man have been viewed from the house at the same moment.

TITHE All tithes are payable by the owner; in all they amount to about £5 2s 4d per annum.

28

2018

Folly builders are invariably rich romantics. The kind that would choose to inhabit a summit like this, no longer exist. After failing to sell in 1925, the Kearleys leased to a syndicate who continued the shoots, and they came back for a few further visits, but eventually stopped. They were often spoken of, and still are mentioned occasionally, but nowadays people know or remember little. This much is known: Hudson's business partner Gilbert Tonge died with no heir and Hudson, finding that his own children were not business-minded, sold the business before his own death. Selina died in 1931, and Hudson followed in 1934, both in the same place, on their new estate in Scotland. Their children have since passed away too. Gerald became the second Viscount Devonport. He came back to visit as an old man a few years before his own death. He was saddened to see me as a shelter for sheep. He had been thinking of me for a while, especially after Beryl passed. She never did marry nor have children, and it is probable that she carried her secret to the grave, though her life was not without some happiness. Gerald and Mark both married and had families. Mark moved to Canada where he became an official artist of the Second World War in Esquimalt. He was involved in the art scene in Victoria and was the last of the family to pass on, in 1977.

After the Thomases left, a local family owned me. By then, the land was more attractive than a derelict mansion. I was stripped of anything of value and left thereafter to the elements. People trespassed in order to visit and some came to steal whatever they could. There was a glimmer of hope when two young men offered cash to buy me for a themed hotel project. They were refused.

A young family, who were close neighbours, often visited from 1979 onwards, and the two girls scratched their names onto fallen slates. On one occasion they wrote their name and the year, 1981, which reminded me of someone. They looked in the windows, but their mother, carrying a baby brother told them not to go in. By then, the upper floors had fallen through and the grand staircase was blocked by debris.

'If you go in there, you could be killed,' said their father. 'The walls will be next.' So they walked around me instead. Clockwise. They posed and took photos standing on the steps. They brought their relatives from London to see me and someone said, this is like paradise; but they were looking at the purple heather. At that time, I made music in the hills as the wind rushed through my hollow shell. I could play a few different notes depending on wind direction and speed. It was an impressive sound, like a giant horn, and it made the younger girl scream. 'It's a ghost!' she cried. I thought it mournful and it carried a goodly distance; not that there were many there to hear it.

At what point does a house become a ruin? I am not sure if it was that moment when the Thomases left and Alis in her bobble hat, carrying a battered suitcase, did not give a second glance as she walked out to the waiting vehicles. It was Gwen who turned around and walked backwards for a while. Her long hair streaming in the wind and her arms wrapped around herself. She often did that when she needed comforting. She still had the necklace with the blue locket, although she had replaced the lock of Owen's hair with the fox tooth. Dewi glanced back too, but briefly. Gwen was still looking from the window of the car as they drove away.

Or was it when the man came to steal the lead? That was the beginning of real decline. I was inundated with water from then on and though the thief was caught and imprisoned, no repairs were done thereafter.

Rain entered, soaking the beams, the walls and floorboards. Wallpaper peeling away was the least of the problems. The roof collapsed as the wood rotted and the wind that now entered caught hold of anything that was loose and pulled at it, toying with it as a child would, though there was nothing child-like about the hands of the wind.

There was no one here the night a storm took down most of the north wall, the one where Owen hid a letter and vainly hoped that Beryl would find it. The chimney that Alis once climbed was one of the first to go. The last chimney fell in the nineties. The one that Gwen liked to sit by.

The frontal east-facing walls have proven the sturdiest. They shore up piles of broken bones. The stone archway to the grand entrance is still intact. No upper walls remain but it's possible to see most of the footprint still. People often have their photographs at the front door, standing on the rubble that buries the steps, with a hill of bricks, beams, stone and plaster behind them. Now that I am little more than a collapsed mess, they take more pictures than ever before, holding their glinting screens up and smiling into them.

But it is mostly quiet here now. Grouse walk by sometimes, cautiously, as if they expect one of the ghosts that slaughtered their forebears. The greening of the piles of stone, brick, metal and wood is the final stage in my interment. Enough dirt has gathered to begin to create a soil, allowing grass and moss to grow on the rubble hill; perhaps heather will take root and bloom here too.

For my part, I prefer not to observe too much of my decline, but to remain happily in the early part of the last century with the people who lived here then. In times to come, I will disappear beneath the hill leaving a few mysterious stones for visitors to wonder at. The winds will blow as they always have, but without the power to harm me.

🐚 Author's Note:

Readers will have guessed by now, that fiction has mixed with fact here, as it inevitably must when writing a historical novel of this sort. While the stories of Hudson Kearley and David Lloyd George follow factual accounts closely, the story of Beryl Kearley is a fictionalised account, although it is true that Hudson and Selina had a daughter named Beryl, and it does appear that she did not marry or have children. Similarly the events of 1954 are fiction. There was indeed a family living at Gwylfa Hiraethog at that time and they did leave in 1954, but the Thomas family are imaginary and bear no intended resemblance to them.

A free eBook on the history of the house, with photos and local stories about Gwylfa Hiraethog, will be released later this year. For more information, you can sign up to my newsletter through my website at https://rachelvknox.wordpress.com or follow my author page (Rachel V Knox - Author) on Facebook.

If you have stories or photos of Gwylfa Hiraethog to offer for inclusion in the book, please do get in touch.

Acknowledgements:

Extracts of Lloyd George's speech at Gwylfa Hiraethog, courtesy of *Denbighshire Free Press*, 5th September 1908.

Estate Agent Particulars – Adapted from records, courtesy of The National Library of Wales, Aberystwyth.

Thanks to Holly Knox for editorial work and many useful suggestions.

Thanks to Eira Jones for her historical talk and information on life at Gwylfa Hiraethog.

Hudson Ewbanke Kearley's privately published memoir, *The Road Travelled, Some Memories of a Busy Life,* gave details on his political and business life, and on the motoring trip to France.

Gwylfa Hiraethog
August, 2017

© R Knox